THE LAST
TOUR

A THRILLER

GLENN A. BRUCE

This is a work of fiction. Names, characters, places, and incidents are products of the author's imagination or are used fictitiously and are not to be construed as real. Any resemblance to actual events, locations, organizations, or persons, living or dead, is entirely coincidental.

World Castle Publishing, LLC
Pensacola, Florida
Copyright © Glenn A. Bruce 2023
Hardback ISBN: 9798395061676
Paperback ISBN: 9781960076786
eBook ISBN: 9781960076793
First Edition World Castle Publishing, LLC, June 19, 2023
http://www.worldcastlepublishing.com
Licensing Notes
Cover: Karen Fuller
Editor: Karen Fuller

1

Marion Cooper had not wanted to come halfway around the world with her husband Dan for an impromptu vacation, but things had gotten bumpy between the two in the last year, and she feared letting him go on his own. Who knew what might happen.

Whom he might meet.

For his part, Dan had suggested Alaska come February, Detroit now — "It's getting better, really — just the water, still" — or yet *another* cruise around the western Caribbean at Christmas. Marion gave easy-to-say "No thanks" to all three.

So Phnongtuk it was.

Though Dan had assured his wife that he would be fine on his own and would return in a better mood all around, he failed to convince Marion to let out his leash. Too many near-fights and uncomfortably silent movie nights at home.

Netflix, no chill.

Marion was not naïve; she knew that eighteen childless years could put a strain on any couple. So discretion became the better part of a valorous *No, you go on without me, I'll see you in three weeks,* and she took over booking the tour.

She found a hotel a few blocks off the beach with a slice of a view from their balcony at a reasonable price for peak season. Anticipating crowds from around the Southern Asian basin, as Dan referred to it, Marion delighted in discovering that the first five days of their vacation would fall on a Kurchin holiday, so they might get some relief from the hordes. As it turned out, the beaches were nearly empty—just enough Australians to chat up when company became a yearning.

On the final day of the local spiritual holiday, Dan and Marion strolled the vacant shore knowing that the next day would see throngs of natives taking their annual mid-summer work-break, a national holiday to follow the austere religiosity of the preceding week.

"That's a nice custom," Marion said, dragging her bare foot in the sugary white sand.

"Hmm?" Dan said.

"I said, requiring a week of partying after a week of Asian Lent is a nice idea. Kind of a reverse Fat Tuesday."

"I don't think it's required," he said.

Marion put her hand on her husband's arm. "Dan."

He stopped with her. "Yes?"

"Not that you've been a bundle of fun this week, but today...." She paused. "Is everything okay? Are you upset with me?"

Dan Cooper looked almost surprised. "No," he said. "Not at all. I promise." He gave her hand a squeeze.

"Because you seem even more distant than—"

"I've got a lot on my mind," he said.

"Such as?" Marion said.

"Work, you know. The usual," he said, shrugging while

looking out across the water as if expecting a sea creature to rise.

Marion looked but saw nothing, so she said, "I thought things were going well at the office."

"They are," he said.

"And you're still up for that promotion, right? The raise?" Marion Cooper was not a gold digger, and her question reflected that indifference to money. Her concern focused exclusively on her mate. Was he getting what he wanted and deserved? Was he happy at work? At home? Their house and life were more than comfortable, plenty enough for a farm girl from Nebraska — if one with a PhD. in Indigenous Cultures of the West.

Dan said, "Oh yeah, sure. I think Morgan's pretty locked into bumping me up — no matter what Phil Atters has to say about it."

"Phil," Marion chuckled in a way that said, *That asshole.* Then, she went back to, "So?"

Dan did his version of hemming and hawing and said, "Just the usual politics."

Marion wondered, "Did something go wrong in Kiev?"

"No," Dan said. "It was fine." He always said he felt bad not being able to tell his wife the full details about his business trips, but he was bound by certain international agreements and NDAs with his employer. Plus, he allowed that she would find it exceedingly dull. "Nuts and bolts stuff," he always said.

"It was complicated," Dan finally volunteered. "The whole thing is...complicated." When Marion did not ask how, he said, "These IMF deals, trying to work in global support for underprivileged communities — whole countries — while bolstering share values and guaranteeing dividends...."

"Tricky business," Marion said. "Why don't you consider retirement, Dan? Seriously."

Dan snapped a look.

"I know, I know," Marion said. "But you've put in your twenty—plus—and I don't see you enjoying it anymore. Quite frankly, you seem…miserable at times."

Dan checked the ocean again and, without looking at Marion, said, "I can't just walk away in the middle of a project. *Projects*. Morgan and Phil would be lost."

"Well," Marion said, trying to stay upbeat and supportive. "You're the man for the job—whether you want it or not. Morgan is happy to have you at the helm of that operation. Phil, too, I suppose."

"Sure," Dan said, "if I wasn't, his fat ass would be here instead of mine."

Marion retrieved her hand. Her tone soured. "I thought this was a vacation. *Only* a vacation."

Dan looked away.

"Oh, Dan. Good Christ," Marion said. "Can we not go *anywhere* without your office in the suitcase. In your *head*."

She thumped his temple with her index finger—then turned away.

Dan sighed. "Marion, I'm…." he said. "It's just—"

"It's just what, Dan?" Marion said, spinning back. "Your work interfering in everything we do? Everywhere we go? There's you, there's me, and there's Kasner International."

"It's not that bad."

"It's not that bad?" Marion said, allowing her jaw to drop. "Dan, they're in our cars, on our phones, in our closets. In our *bed*."

"That's not true," Dan said.

"They're in your head," Marion said, and thumped his temple again. "So yes, they're everywhere we go."

"I wish you'd stopped doing that," Dan said.

Marion said, "I don't know any other way to get through to you. You ignore every attempt to talk about it. Telling me, 'Oh, it's just work. Don't worry about it.' 'It's boring.' Well, I *am* worried, Dan. I've very worried. Your work has come between us since…since I've *known* you. On our first date, you excused yourself from the table to call Joshua Morgan to 'check in.'"

Marion turned away in frustration. Then back. "For fuck's sake, Dan. You're more married to him and Kasner than you are to me."

Marion walked a small circle and came back to give her ultimatum. "I've had it. Okay? Either you are here with me these next few days, or you are with your work. Your choice. But if you choose Door Number Two, this is our last tour — and when we get back, we are having a serious discussion about where we go from here. And I don't mean back to Georgetown, so don't even try. Okay?"

Marion stared at her silent husband a moment longer, then said, "I need a drink," and headed for the nearest tiki bar.

2

By the time Dan Cooper had taken in enough of the primal cerulean beauty of the Phnongtuk beachside reef and walked over to join his wife on the stool next to her at the tiki bar, she was on her second Cootie, a local specialty drink popular with tourists.

Dan told the bartender, "Johnny Blue, rocks."

"You got it, boss," the young man said — barely more than a boy, Dan thought — and headed for the top shelf.

After a moment of silence, Marion said, "I'm sorry, Dan. That was over the top."

"No," he said. "You're right. I'm not good at balancing this work/marriage thing. I need to get better at it. Without threats."

Marion sighed as if subverting renewed anger. "I wasn't threatening you."

"Yes, you were," Dan said. "And I deserve it. I'm the one who needs to apologize, not you."

Marion ran the brightly-patterned swizzle stick around her luscious adult beverage — fruity but with an imperious kick — to get her thoughts mixed as well as her drink, then said,

"I appreciate that. I do. But I have not been the best wife, either."

"Don't say that," he said.

"No, I need to," she said. "Dan, there's something I—"

"Hey, Americans!"

The voice came from behind Dan.

He spun. If the young couple had known him, they would have recognized that Dan was startled at how he had not noticed their approach—not like him at all—as he said, "Yeah. Maryland. We're kind of having a—"

Before Dan could say "private conversation here," the young man, a blond surfer type in his mid-twenties, said, "Illinois via California, where Alanda here is from. We met at school in Tulsa—don't even ask about that—and the rest is, as they say, happy history."

"How do you do?" Alanda, his pretty Black bride said, formally. She obviously had a more formal upbringing than her husband. "My rude husband is Lucas Tucker, of the La Jolla Tuckers—the *laid-back* ones, obviously—and I am Alanda, formerly of the Oak Park Borsombs—though we were usually referred to as the Boredoms, because we are, well…."

She let it hang.

Caught in a socializing net set by her *own* formal upbringing, Marion said, "I'm Marion, and this is my husband, Dan."

"Of the Bethesda Dans," he said, somewhat caustically.

"Dan," Marion turned back. "Be nice. Please."

Dan said nothing but waved his empty glass at the bartender. The young man nodded and darted for the good stuff. He recognized Dan and Marion from the day before as good tippers despite a loose law against it in Phnongtuk.

Young Lucas raised his voice in that direction. "Hey, if

you don't mind, could we get a couple of those Cootie things. You make 'em the best on the beach."

"Yessir," the boy said, and reached for the Cootie mix while pouring Dan's scotch.

Lucas turned back to tell the Coopers, "We're newlyweds if you hadn't guessed."

Marion said, "Yes, I could tell by your lack of a tan."

Lucas scrunched up his blond features while his new wife translated for him, "We haven't been out of the room much."

"Oh! Yeah, that," he said, blushing. "I guess not." Then he said, defensively, "We took a tour of the Valley."

"That we did," Alanda said, smiling. "And then…."

"Back to our room," Lucas said, shyly turning his face to the sand.

"Sounds lovely, actually," Marion said, with the briefest of glances at her husband—saved when the bartender brought the two Cooties, plus another for Marion and the Blue Label.

Marion saw her fresh drink and started to say, "I didn't—"

"On the house, ma'am. You folks have been most kind to me. It's the least I could do." He smiled and turned away.

Marion said, "He's so nice—and well-spoken for…here."

Dan nodded, his eyes peeled keenly on their bartender.

Marion had a pang of guilt. She turned to Alanda. "That sounded awful, didn't it?"

"No," Alanda said breezily. "I was thinking the same thing."

Lucas had been watching the ocean, probably thinking about surfing, when he turned back to ask, "So, Dan. What do you do for a living?"

Marion turned to her husband. "Yes, Dan. What *do* you do for a living?"

Dan gave her a respectful smile and told Lucas, "International finance, in a sense. Around metals and hardware, copper mostly."

"Sounds exciting," Lucas said, sarcastically—but not mean.

"It isn't," Dan assured him.

As Lucas nodded, Alanda wondered, "What does that entail, exactly?"

Marion said, "Exactly?" as she finished her second Cootie and started in on her third, looking over her straw at her husband with eyes wide. "*Dan?*"

"You might wanna go easy on those," Dan suggested. "They've got more oomph than they claim."

"That's why I like 'em," Marion said.

Lucas said, "Oomph," with a chuckle—as if enjoying the grandparents.

Dan smiled wanly.

Marion said to the young couple. "Day drinking. It's the reason for the season. The libation of the vacation. The pause for the cause. And…whatever else anyone wants to add."

She held up her drink for a toast and clunked plastic glasses with Alanda, who said, happily, "I'll drink to that."

Lucas said, "Me too. And I didn't understand a word of it." He happily toasted and drank his Cootie in one gulp.

Their bartender set to mixing two more. Lucas saw that and said, "This place is awesome. The weather is perfect, the people are totally cool—and there's no tipping. How great is *that*?" He smiled at the bar boy as he delivered two Cooties. The young bartender returned a faint semblance and returned to his station.

Dan said, somewhat darkly, "You're paying for it one way

or another."

Marion said, "Oh, Dan. Let them enjoy their honeymoon, for godsake. Loosen up." She turned back to the kids. "My husband, the hardworking spoilsport."

Dan looked out to sea again.

Alanda grinned at Lucas. "That's us in ten years," she said. Then she wondered, "How many years have you guys been married?"

Marion said, "I'd say 'too many,' but Dan would throw me in the ocean."

Lucas said, "At least it's warm," and his wife elbowed him.

Dan said, "Eighteen married, twenty-three together. And no, not too many at all." His almost-smile was met with the same from Marion.

Alanda said, "Well, I think you make a lovely couple. Well-matched. That's my impression—for what it's worth."

Marion said, "That's worth a lot, thank you," and turned to Dan to find him…staring at a thirty-five-ish blonde in a skimpy top, showing ample cleavage, and low-slung sarong, showing where her pubic hair would have been if she had any.

The woman said to Dan, "See something you like, sailor?"

Marion's face went flat, and she said, "Are you selling?"

The woman said, "If you're buying." She swayed slightly, apparently already having enjoyed her own day-drinking *binge*.

Lucas's grin was about to break his face. Alanda elbowed him, but she eyed the new woman—and crossed her legs nervously.

The woman stuck her hand out to Marion and said, "Lana Yarborough, A-R-C." She pointed up to the lone factory looming on the hill above. "Covering the world in cardboard, one box at a time. Woohoo!"

Alanda said, "You work there?"

"As little as possible, honey. May I?" She was asking about mounting the stool between the couples — *as* she was mounting it. She said, "When my boss asked if I wanted to transfer here, I was thinking beautiful beaches, sexy tourists, hot times in almost-Thailand." She scoffed. "Then *this*."

Lucas asked in disbelief, "You don't like it here?"

"Fuckin' hellhole," Lana said with a look to match her tone.

Alanda shifted away on her stool.

"In what way?" Marion wondered.

"*Every* way," Lana said. "Everyone hates everyone else, they can't decide on a religion, and their stupid war never ends." She poured the remainder of her drink down and waved at the bar boy in a way that confirmed why "they" did not like Ugly Americans here — even if she was far from ugly.

The bartender poured her a straight-up bourbon and brought it over. "Thank you, Chachi." She raised her glass at the young man and poured it back. Drained it and muttered, "Whatever the fuck your name is."

Alanda and Lucas shared an unamused millennial glare. Then Lucas said, "There's a war here?"

Lana grunted, then said, "Luke, there's shit going on here...." She waved her hand around generally. "I mean, here. Right here. All around us. Even now, at this moment. Shit, you would not believe if I told you. If I *could* tell you. Fuckin' disaster. Ready to boil over at any instant. Goddamn volcano of chaos. Right here."

When the young bartender brought her another bourbon, neat, Lana grabbed it out of his hand and downed it one gulp as

Alanda asked, "Are we safe?"

"Fuck no," Lana said.

Dan said, "Maybe you've had enough for one day."

"Fuck off, Dan," Lana said. "How do you put up with him?" she asked Marion.

"Sometimes it's a challenge," Marion said honestly, then stood and turned to her husband. "What say we head back to the room?"

"Not so quick, lovebirds," Lana said.

Alanda was still contemplating their safety. "But we're *Americans*."

"Shit, honey," Lana said. "That's even worse." She waved her empty glass at the bar boy, but this time he ignored her.

"Fine," Lana said, and slammed her glass on the bar, telling Alanda, "Look, we did it to ourselves. Meddling all over the goddam world. Going in where we weren't invited. Being general assholes—I mean, 'imperialists.'" She looked to Dan. "Same shit, right, Dan? Different day, different country, same old shit."

Dan stared her down a long moment, then told his wife, "Yeah, I think it's time."

Lana jumped up and intercepted them as they started to turn away. "Hey, wait. What say we all go up to my apartment for some Love, American Style. You know, group-wise. I've got a hot tub that will accommodate everybody. Yeah?"

She looked at the younger couple.

Alanda looked terrified. "Um, we really need to be going, too," she said and stood.

Lana told her, "Newlyweds, right? Always something to do." She made a face to indicate inside knowledge of their lusty plans. Then she turned to Dan and Marion. "Not like when you've been together twenty-three years."

Marion bristled. "Were you listening to *everything* we said?"

"Oh, don't get your panties in a bunch, Mare. I've got, like, 20/10 hearing. I can hear a flea fart in Bangkok from here. And that's what?" She pretended to calculate. "At least ten, twenty miles."

It was closer to five-hundred.

"It's a joke, guys! Come on!" Lana said. "I have great hearing, really. Occupational hazard."

"In cardboard," Dan said—and started to lead Marion away.

Lana jumped in their way again. "Okay," she said as if caving in. "You can play, too. I've got nothing against boys." She sidled up to Marion. "As long as we get our special time."

She rubbed the hair on Marion's forearm.

"Oooo," she said. "I like a little fuzz on a woman." Then she partially recanted, "As long as it's not too much." She raised her eyebrows, then turned to leer at Alanda—who was now clutching Lucas tightly.

Lucas, who was apparently imagining what Lana was suggesting—clearly.

Alanda elbowed him again. He said, "What? I was just...." He did not finish.

Marion, with practiced ice in her umbrage, said to Lana, "Are you really that bored?"

Lana said, "No. But I really am that good."

Marion stood her ground. So, Lana leaned close so that only Marion could hear and said, "I know what you were about to tell him. I can spot a switch-hitter from a mile away." She pulled away with an evil grin crossing her mien.

Marion slapped her!

Dan said, "Marion!"

"She's been following us, Dan! How else...."

Marion stopped. If she went any farther, she might have to continue her confession right here, in front of Lana and the newlyweds.

Alanda said, "We have to go. *Now*, Lucas."

Lana grabbed her arm to stop her. Alanda looked terrified, and Dan looked ready to step in. But Lana said, "No, no, no. You're right. My fault. Sorry. I'm drunk and being stupid. That friend you have to throw out of her own living room. My bad. Forget me and everything I said. I thought you were somebody else — somebody I knew from...somewhere. Else."

Everyone stared.

She turned to Lucas and Alanda. "Have a nice honeymoon, you two." Then to Dan and Marion, "And you guys...."

A beat.

Then she just waved, turned, and started away.

Everyone heaved a sigh of relief — their eyes on the retreating *nutcase* as she staggered across the boulevard for town, causing Lucas to say, "Wow, she really is hammered." He chuckled.

But when Lana stumbled again, Dan said, "Did you feel that?"

Marion said, "The crass hatefulness for everything good about life?"

The ground shook again.

3

Alanda said, "Is that...an earthquake?"

The word barely fell out of her mouth when a tremendous BOOM! sounded, and the beach began shuddering. As the shaking increased, bottles rattled behind the bar, slamming into each other so hard that they began to crack and burst, high-priced liquor flowing like a waterfall onto the lesser brands until the rear wall of the tiki bar shook so hard it simply fell away.

Seeing it go, Dan yanked Marion and Alanda from under the collapsing thatched roof and its log-beam rafters—narrowly.

Being young and athletic, Lucas moved quickly—giving directions like a true San Diegan. "Stay away from walls or anything tall," he told his new wife, who looked terrified. She had never been in a tumbler before.

Across the beach highway, buildings started swaying, windows already shattering. Light poles pitched, powerlines slapped, and transformers exploded like Rolling Thunder. The beach began undulating more than the ocean.

Marion asked, "Why is everyone running for town?"

Lucas's answer was precise. "Stupid."

Dan had another notion. He looked to the sea — and saw it coming.

"Tsunami!" he said abruptly. "High ground. Go!"

He grabbed Marion and started for the highway at a full run — all of them sneaking a look back at the ten-foot wall of water racing toward the sand from several hundred yards out.

"Fuck!" Lucas said — and not because he wished he had his shortboard. He grabbed Alanda and started after Dan and Marion.

Alanda said, "Where are we going? We'll get crushed!"

On the run, Lucas said, "If we stay here, we'll drown!"

As they raced under the swaying palms onto the heaving highway, Dan scanned for the safest escape route. "This way," he decided and, Marion's hand in his, ran for the widest street between the shortest buildings.

Lucas dragged Alanda along without question.

Eighteen seconds had passed — seconds that seemed like minutes — as the rumbling increased, now sounding like a dozen freight trains passing overhead, though the sound pulsed all around them. Explosions came from all sides, and smoke rose.

Fire — already.

A score of shops exploded apart as if detonated from within or crushed by God's random thumb, sending glass, construction materials, canned goods, and souvenirs everywhere. Kitsch rained down like Mardi Gras beads.

Potential victims stumbled out of collapsing hotels, over buckling asphalt and concrete, panicked, racing in all directions, many injured and bleeding. The scene felt surreal, like a rehearsed stunt recreation on a Universal Studios tour.

Even Dan thought it did not look real — and he had experienced a 6.5 in Japan.

More buildings fell. Light poles crashed into each other, their wires interlacing, looking like giant sparklers, raining fire. Cars changed course as the ground lifted beneath them or parted. Every street corner had fender-benders; some had pileups.

Two taxis were hurled through the air like Matchbox toys into a hotel wall that collapsed. Another ended up into a tree. Bodies spilled out onto the pavement. Blood spread as the throbbing booms continued.

Marion said, "It sounds like we're under attack!"

Dan stopped to get his bearings, checking back to see that the ocean had crossed the beach and was now shoving up across the boulevard.

The others saw it, too.

Alanda started screaming, and even Lucas froze. "Where do we go!" Half the town seemed to have been demolished already. Fires blazed everywhere, smoke getting thick, wreckage all about.

"This way," Dan shouted over the tumult, rerouting into a rare empty lot free of flying debris—seawater already edging across the street onto the bare soil.

In those few seconds, as they reached the top of the gently sloping field, the wave reached it as well—pushing in. Now, Dan was worried. "Fuck."

Which way to go?

The only answer was to continue, "Up." So up they ran as the ocean began lapping at their heels. But around the next corner, they found themselves boxed in. No exit. Nowhere to run. The water rushing for them. No way to retreat.

Here they would die.

As the swirling ocean reached their knees, Alanda sagged, sobbing. Giving up one's life, knowingly, is not easy at twenty-three. Lucas cried with her, and they hugged.

Dan's eyes flew wide with knowing dread—when he caught Marion's, still as an Alpine pond on a warm summer day and as blue. Only the hint of a tear giving away her sense of coming loss. All she said—all she had to say, "I love you."

At that moment, all was forgiven; all was forgotten.

Marion stretched up to give Dan a gentle parting kiss on his familiar lips—

"This way! Come on! Hurry!"

The familiar voice came from above. They all looked to find Lana bent down over the wall above, holding on with one hand to the railing behind her. She appeared calm, determined—and sober.

All Marion could say was, "Her."

The roar of a rising tide obscured the dismay in her voice as the water climbed up around their waists as all eyes turned up, hopeful, desperate.

"Give me your hand," Lana said to Alanda—who dove without question for the extended helping hand and grabbed it tightly. With one strong yank, Lana had the thin girl out of the water and shoved her up onto the concrete ledge above them, even as chunks of the cement fell into the rising water.

Dan imagined drowning in an aquarium. As much as he held some trace of hope that they might rise with the water to safety, he knew tsunamis did not treat their victims gently—rather, thrashing and drowning, beaten into submission.

Sinking to die.

Lucas went next. As Lana helped him up past her, she had the presence of mind to say, "So much for chivalry," and extended her hand to, "Marion. Come on."

All mistrust left as Marion, now clavicle-deep in dirty

seawater, reached up and clasped tightly, Dan shoving her butt—in the process, freeing her waterlogged flowered sarong.

Too much weight.

The water rose to Dan's neck, then over his nose, then his head—in seconds—underwater currents pulling him in every direction at once as he kept his hand above his head, swinging it around, hoping for contact.

"Hold still," Lana said, grabbing at her moving target.

"Help him. Please," Marion heard herself say. And, "Lucas?" Turning to him.

Wet and disoriented, Lucas saw and flipped over the railing, getting hold of Dan's flailing hand.

"Help me!" Lucas cried out. "I can't hold him!"

Lana lowered herself closer to the rising tide to latch onto Dan's wrist. She and Lucas heaved for all they were worth to lift a gasping Dan from the angry, rising waters in one move, up onto the narrow ledge, then shoving him up over the railing—almost falling back in, themselves.

Now Marion and Alanda helped, pulling their rescuer and Lucas up to relative safety as Dan gasped for liquid-free air, choking, coughing.

"Up," Lana said, lifting him to his feet—Dan following orders without contest as he knew, despite his soggy brain and aching lungs, that this was just the beginning of their flight.

If they were lucky.

Lana led the group horizontally, along the slight incline that allowed glimpses down streets leading to the sea where cars were being shoved into heaps, people in them panicked and screaming.

Dying.

More buildings came apart, walls falling, poles tilting into the water, electrocuting anyone unlucky enough to have lived to reach that point.

Bodies already floated in groups.

As the water topped the wall and reached Dan's knees, he shouted, "We need to get higher!"

Lana said, "Two more blocks," as water grabbed at their thighs.

"We won't last two more blocks," Dan said.

Lana took a quick look down then ahead and decided he was right. "Okay. Here." She turned into — another dead end.

"Shit!" Lucas shouted. Then he saw the old stone stairs — impossibly steep and narrow, with the buildings on both sides collapsing down around them. "We won't make it!" he shouted, wide-eyed. "It's too steep!"

"Would you rather stay here?" Lana said — wood, coconuts, and beach chairs pounding into their legs on the still-rising tidal bore.

Without waiting for an answer, she started up the stairs just as the tops of the two buildings swayed to meet in the middle and loosed a barrage of bricks, one of them hitting Lana on the side of her head and shoulder. She went down.

Dan reflexively reached to grab her, but she shoved up on her own. "I'm okay."

She did not look okay. Blood streamed from a cut on the side of her head onto her already-bruising bare shoulder.

When she saw Alanda staring at the blood, Lana shoved her ahead. "Don't look. Just run. Up the steps. Go."

Alanda obeyed, and Lana said, "Marion, you're up. Go!"

Marion did not question the command. She jogged up three steps, took Alanda's hand in hers, and the two helped each other ahead and up the steep-hewn stairs, using the walls on either side to keep them from falling as the occasional chunk of mortar clunked down around them.

Lana did not have to tell Lucas to go. He was two steps below Alanda and Marion, moving as quickly as he could. Lana then Dan followed.

The second temblor struck.

The stones below Lana and Dan fell out from under them, and both dropped straight down—just grabbing hold of the twisted handrails on either side of the stairs.

Dangling.

Dan told her, "Hang on. I got you."

"No! You go," Lana told him with the first hint of emotion she had shown. "Save yourself. Get your wife."

Dan looked up briefly. Marion and Alanda were almost to the top of the steep, narrow steps. He looked back. "If I swing my legs around you, can you climb up me?"

"No," she said.

"No, you can't, or no, you won't?" he said.

"No, just—" She stopped herself. "Okay."

"Here we go," Dan said. "One...." He kicked out and swung a little "Two...." Another kick, a longer swing and....

The *three* was silent.

He got his legs around Lana's waist just as her side of the wall let go, crumbling away into the still-rising waters—swinging her down into the melee of crashing waves and junk.

"Hold on!" Dan shouted, no fear of showing fear. "Jesus!"

He struggled to hold on to Lana and the railing.

Higher up, Marion, Alanda, and Lucas reached the top landing and turned to look down, no doubt expecting to see Lana and Dan right behind them.

They saw Dan barely hanging on to a dangling piece of

pipe, mostly torn loose from the stuccoed wall—and Lana on him, her arms wrapped around his neck, naked from the waist down, having lost her sarong.

No bottoms.

Marion did not have time to notice or care. "Hold on!" she shouted down, quickly joined by the others. "HOLD ON! HOLD ON!"

Not that anyone could hear over the cacophony—the continuing booms like incoming artillery, the rush of waves, the rumbling of temblors beneath the earth's crust—but it did not matter. Lana was not *about* to let go.

Or not crack a joke. "Is that a life-preserver in your pocket, or are you just happy to see me?"

"Get off!" Dan said. "Go!"

Not in the mood.

With surprising strength again, Lana pulled herself up Dan's body, grinding her exposed parts into his face. "That was a freebie," she said but did not stop.

"Get...off...me," Dan sputtered, feeling his own strength waning. "I can't...hold on...much—"

A second later, Lana was on a solid step, pulling him up. "Straight and easy," she said.

Two seconds after that, Dan stood beside her on the last remaining bottom step, staring at her bareness.

"You always go around like that?" he said, dourly.

"I call it dressing for success," she said, and turned to run up the steps ahead of him. Though he did not want to look, Dan could not help himself.

After what they had just been through, he deserved a reward. After all, he had just saved her life.

Or had she saved his?

4

Lana unlocked the door to her apartment and let everyone in.

The place was plain, spartan even—no hot tub—but thankfully high and dry, well above the tsunami madness, and had not sustained any observable damage.

"American-built," she said. "I'll give ARC that much."

"No cardboard," Dan said.

"Just cardboard money," Lana said—and quickly looked through her rooms.

"Expecting someone," Marion said, ruffled again.

"Just being sure. You never know with these heathens."

"Speaking of which," Marion said, "would you mind?"

She nodded down at Lana's half-nakedness.

Lucas gawked openly as if he had just now noticed. Alanda elbowed him again.

Lana looked down. "Forgot. Sorry." She started for her bedroom and turned back to add, "Really. I mean…who knew we'd have an earthquake and a tsunami, and who the fuck knows what all else?"

She went into her bedroom—and closed the door!

Marion looked at her husband. "What does she mean by that?" Dan shrugged as if he had no clue. So Marion rode him a bit. "Enjoy your little rescue?"

"Most fun I've had almost dying in as long as I can remember."

"Hmmm," his wife said.

Lana returned quickly, wearing short-shorts and a fresh, dry t-shirt, her hair up in a ponytail—carrying a Glock 9mm.

"What's that for?" Lucas asked.

"Looters," Dan said.

"What he said," Lana said—and went to discreetly peer out her window, being careful to stay off to one side, behind the vertical blinds.

Alanda asked, "What are you looking for?"

Dan said, "Desperate throngs."

Lana said, "Again."

Marion said, "You two working together?"

"Yeah," her husband said. "We're opening at Caesar's on the Ides of March."

"Three weeks. All the slots we can lose our money in," Lana said.

Lucas chuckled. "You two are funny."

Marion scowled.

Apparently deciding it was safe to be at the windows, Lana told everyone to, "Have a look."

They all edged to the windows to look down—and gasped. Entire blocks of the town were gone, bare foundations under swirling water—which seemed to have reached its peak tidal surge but had yet to begin receding.

As they watched a few last locals coming out of an access hatch onto a roof—the entire building collapsed into the still-swirling waters, taking everything and everyone with it.

"Oh my god!" Alanda wailed, turning away. Crying instantly. "Those poor people." She looked unstable and said, "I think I'm going to be sick."

"Bathroom's in there," Lana said, pointing. Then, "Lucas! Bathroom."

He was still staring at the window in shock. "Huh?"

"She's going to be sick," Marion said. "Please help her."

"Who?" Lucas said, bewildered.

"Your *wife*," Dan said and pointed. "She needs help to the bathroom."

Lucas looked to see that Alanda had turned a mild shade of green and gone wobbly. "Oh," he said and rushed over, leading her through the bedroom to the bathroom.

They all heard him say, "I'm sorry, baby. I was...it's awful."

Then they heard puking—hard to tell from whom.

Lana said to Dan and Marion, "Well, might as well make yourselves comfortable. We're gonna be here a while."

She opened a pantry. "I've got plenty of stores to last until the water goes down—which, well, come to think of, it won't be that long. The real problem's gonna be the typhus and dysentery after, of course, looting, and god knows what these fucking people will do."

Though she seemed to be talking more to herself than her guests, Dan and Marion listened, exchanging looks of concern—Marion silently conveying that she would like Dan to speak up.

He did. "We should probably see if our hotel made it. It's up the hill, too. Just...." He waved his hand generally to the left. "Over there, ten blocks or so."

"The Tiger Tree," Lana said.

Marion said, "How did you know that?"

Lana said, "Popular tourist haunt; you two look the type," seemingly without a thought. "But I doubt Mr. Krinh will be able to feed all of his guests. In the meantime…."

She pointed at her full pantry as Lucas and Alanda returned and….

BAMM! Another temblor?

Everyone braced for the building to start swaying. Instead….

The door crashed in, having been kicked, and armed soldiers poured into the small room. So, of course….

Lana shot one of them. Lucky for her, she hit Kevlar.

He and two others moved on her before she could get another shot off — beating her down and taking her Glock — while the other men shouted in their native language, waving their guns around, giving orders no one could understand, and scaring the shit out of Alanda.

She fainted.

"What the fuck—" was all Lucas got out as he moved quickly for her and got a gun butt to his neck for it.

The soldiers came at Dan and Marion.

Deciding it was time to try the universal plea under such circumstances, Dan stepped forward, cautiously raising his voice. "Americans. We're Americans."

One of the soldiers seemed to understand enough to shout, "Evacuation! Evacuation!" Though it did not sound exactly like the way English-speaking persons pronounce the word.

Marion asked Dan, "What's he saying?"

"Evacuate," Dan said. "They're probably clearing the area to be safe."

"With assault rifles?" she said.

Dan shrug-nodded as if to say, *We're in no position to argue* — because *of those assault rifles.*

He did not need to mention the hand grenades.

Two soldiers joined in, shouting, "Evacuation! Evacuation! Now go! Evacuation!"

Lana forced herself to her feet, unsteady but resolved to resist. "No! American. A-R-C." She pointed in the general direction of the cardboard plant a hundred yards above them. "Americans. We stay here!"

"Evacuation! Now!" they yelled, ignoring her. So, she tried it in their language, shouting something decisive and clearly not in agreement.

A soldier raised his gun to strike her down, causing Marion to react without thinking. "No!" she shouted, stepping in between the soldier and Lana.

Lana, calm again—in *this.* "Marion, it's okay. We may have to do what they say — or get shot."

"I don't want to go," Marion said, both scared and defiant.

Dan told her, quietly, "Just follow my lead. If we cooperate, no one should get hurt."

Marion looked doubtful.

Lucas had his doubts as well. He stood up. "What the fuck is going on? You assholes can't bust in here and rough us up. We're Americans. A-mer-i-can. On va-ca-tion!"

A soldier stepped at him, gun butt raised, screaming something unintelligible.

"Okay, okay!" Lucas said, holding an arm up for protection and stepping back.

The soldiers waved their weapons toward the door and outside, screaming, "Evacuation! Evacuation! All go now! Evacuation! Go now!"

Marion made her decision—as a question. "Maybe we should go."

Looking to Dan.

Dan made his decision with equal lack of confidence. "They're probably evacuating the whole town to see who made it and begin rescue efforts."

"Maybe we can help," his wife said.

"Yeah, maybe," Dan said—but his eyes stayed on Lana, whose eyes stayed on him.

Alanda, having woken up, rose to her feet unevenly. "What's going on?"

Lucas told her, "They're evacuating the city. You know, because of the quake and the tsunami and all."

"Oh," she said with some relief. "Then we should go. Right?"

"Evacuation! Everyone! Must go now! Evacuation!"

Dan nodded. "I'd say we don't have a choice." He continued looking at Lana—which did not go unnoticed by Marion.

Lana said, flatly, "We're safe here."

Marion said, "You're saying we're not safe out there?"

"EVACUATION! EVACUATION! GO NOW! GO NOW! EVACUATION!"

"I'm saying we're safe in here."

An aftershock rocked the building causing the soldiers to lose what was left of their composure, shouting, "HURRY-HURRY! YOU GO NOW! YOU GO NOW! EVACUATE! NOW!" Their eyes darted around with fear.

Lucas concluded, "They're trying to save us."

Alanda agreed. "We should go before the building collapses."

The soldiers were now swinging their muzzles from

American to American.

Lucas said, "Or before we get fucking shot."

Lana said, with incredible calm, "They won't shoot us in my apartment. ARC has diplomatic immunity. They hurt anyone in here, and they could get executed by their own government."

"They already hurt someone," Lucas said. "You. You're bleeding."

"I was bleeding before," Lana said, still as calm as sipping a mint julep on a front porch in May. "Plus, I did shoot at them first."

Lucas now appeared annoyed. "Yeah, why'd you do that? That's probably why they're so mad."

One of the soldiers suddenly fired two shots into the ceiling, causing everyone to jump.

Alanda said, "I'm going." She started for the door — Lucas with her, clutching her hand — soldiers' guns trained on them.

When they neared the door, the closest soldiers shoved them outside, then turned their muzzles back on the remaining three.

Marion looked at Lana this time. "Do we have a choice?"

Lana did not look like she wanted to, but she shook her head no.

5

The solidly constructed ten-unit apartment building seemed to hang above the still-unfolding chaos, one of four identical buildings clustered along the front edge of a wide flat spot carved into the steep hillside, ARC warehouse perched above.

As the five Americans emerged from Lana's unit, they saw troop carriers coming and going as army jeeps flitted around between and away—the roar of ebbing waters and raging fires filling the air with panic as another small temblor shook the site.

Women screamed.

A soldier led Lucas and Alanda down the stairs into the disorganized frenzy, scared locals and foreigners—ARC employees and lucky tourists who made high ground—shoved and rushed this way and that in no apparent order, despite the continuous shouting of the many armed military types.

Behind the young couple trailed two soldiers from the apartment, then Dan, Marion, and Lana. Behind them, the last two soldiers.

Shouts of, "American! A-R-C!" blended with German, French, and Italian versions of the same as soldiers herded dazed and frightened people up and into the small transport trucks, which then drove off in a hurry.

Marion tried to take in as much detail as she could but found it hopeless. For though the waters seemed to have reached their inland peak, explosions continued, and thick smoke from the fires rolled in like sea fog, limiting visibility to a hundred feet or less and making it hard to breathe.

Someone—maybe a Red Cross worker—shoved a paper mask into her hand and, eyes watering, Marion affixed it to her face as their group melded into the jostling mass of humanity—soldiers running around in the smoke, randomly grabbing residents, taking some one way, others the other, others right into the heart of madness—Marion looked on amazed that no one had gotten run over.

Yet.

The next moment, Marion was the one being grabbed and dragged away. She heard Alanda say, "Marion?" in a tiny, pleading voice.

"It's okay, dear," Marion said—not believing it herself. "Just don't fight them."

"Okay," came the tinier agreement laced with ragged coughing.

Seeing that Alanda had no mask, Marion said, "Here," and took hers off, helping Alanda get it secured on her face as they continued to be herded along.

After thirty feet of being roughhoused, Marion could take no more and pulled away from her captors. "Okay, okay! I can walk on my own!"

When she looked back and saw a soldier all but dragging Alanda, Marion stepped over quickly and pulled his hand off the thin Black girl's arm. "She can walk! Leave her alone!"

The man in green fatigues shouted, "Evacuation! Evacuation!" Pointing ahead with his AK-47.

"For fuck's sake," Marion bitched at no one and everyone and said, with irritation. "Dan, can you help us, here? Please? Dan!" Marion looked to her right.

No, Dan.

To her left. "Dan?"

No, Dan.

Just as Marion realized Dan was no longer with her, loud shouting came just before a roaring rumble, and a large chunk of the hillside let loose.

The mud rushed fast and hungry. Though most in the parking area scrambled out of the way, the enormous glop of sodden earth fully enveloped a troop truck loaded with people. More screams came from those who saw it. Some ran that way.

Reflexively, Marion turned to join them. Her guardian soldier yelled, "No! Evacuation!"

"But we have to help them! There are people in there. Under the mud!"

"Evacuation! Go!"

He herded her with his rifle—jabbing it into her ribs.

"Goddammit! No!" Marion shouted back at him, stopping to stand her ground. "My husband and I will *help*! We need to help those people!"

Seeing no soldiers attempting to dig out the truck— instead pulling and shoving away civilians who tried—Marion tried "Dan! *Dan!*" again.

But Dan was nowhere to be seen.

"Where'd he go?" Marion asked anyone, looking worried for the first time.

Alanda noticed. "What?"

"Dan's gone. I can't find him."

Her own panic growing, Alanda now looked for, "Lucas. Lucas? LUCAS!"

He was not to be seen, either.

Marion scanned as best she could and realized someone else was gone. "Where is that woman?"

Lana — also not visible.

Beginning to panic, they both looked in all directions, Marion seeing a different kind of troop truck — smaller, faster, with mounted guns — tear away in the opposite direction from the other trucks.

Marion managed to say, "Is that —" a split-second before a soldier jabbed her with his gun butt. "Ow! Goddammit!" Marion yelped. "American! Cut that shit out!"

"Evacuation! Evacuation!"

"Jesus fucking Christ. I *know!*"

She shoved the muzzle of his gun away!

Angered, he moved to jab her again. But this time, Marion dodged it and stepped square in a mud puddle. "Thanks," she said of her sandals. They were not Prada, but "They were new."

Bought for her vacation in *paradise.*

More soldiers now physically shoved Marion and Alanda toward a waiting truck that had just sped up and wrenched to a stop — a soldier in back opening the rear flap and hopping down, shouting in his native tongue for the women to get in *now.*

That part was clear.

"Okay. Okay!" Marion shouted at the uniforms. "Where is my husband? My. *Hus-band.*"

"Evacuation! Stop! Go! Now!"

"What?"

Marion felt overwhelmed but managed to keep it

together—unlike Alanda, who started crying again, likely as hard as she ever had. "Lucas?" she wailed piteously.

Two soldiers grabbed her by her arms and lifted her up onto the tailgate "step" — a narrow metal strip welded onto the gate—while another soldier shoved her ass up.

"Lucas!" she cried out again and sat on one of the facing benches in the back, crying.

When the soldiers grabbed Marion, she pulled away. "I can do it myself! Don't touch me again."

This time, it was she who was clearly understood. Rather than yell or assist, they just jutted their rifles at the truck as if to say *Fine, get in there on your own. Now.*

Marion scoffed at them and turned to the truck's tailgate, grabbing the side chain and putting her muddy flat sandal on the narrow ridge that served as a step. Before she could lift herself all the way up into the truck, soldiers were shoving her ass as they had Alanda.

Marion Cooper was not having that. Spinning back to tell them, "Goddammit, keep your damn hands off—"

Her foot slipped off the tailgate ledge.

Marion Cooper came down straight and hard, catching her forehead on the edge of the truck bed. She saw swirling silver lights.

Then blackness.

6

Marion Cooper heard strange sounds all around her—feet scuffling, urgent voices, the snap of plastic and the clinking of metal touching metal. She did not recognize the language, though it had a familiar ring she could not place.

As she opened her eyes, the light felt invasive, hurtful. Her skull ached. She blinked and squinted, trying to get her balance as well as her bearings, only to realize she lay flat on her back.

As her eyes adjusted, she found herself staring up into the peak of a large white tent. She attempted to turn to her right to see more of the tent and what might be under it, but her neck was stiff and sore—hurting nearly as bad as her forehead.

A voice said, "Oh, you're awake. I got back just in time."

The voice sounded familiar, but not until Marion turned her head to her left did she see and recognize Alanda, who said, "I told them you weren't dead."

Her smile was warm, if forced.

"Where...."

Alanda told Marion, "Hospital tent. They put up a small city of them. Red Cross, I think. And the Army."

Marion noticed, "You have blood on you. Are you hurt?"

Alanda looked down at the fresh blood on her shirt. "No. I've been helping." She nodded around, generally.

Only now did Marion have the lucidity to take in the rest of her surroundings. She lifted up as much as she could and was not comforted by what she saw, rows and rows of wounded men, women, and children in the makeshift "hospital" tent—many of them bandaged heavily, some with IVs, some moaning, some silent.

One getting the sheet pulled up over her face by a local in bloodied green scrubs.

Looking further, Marion could now see a few others with their faces covered—one being carried out on a stretcher by two struggling small men.

Loved ones crying.

Marion looked back at Alanda with a furrowed brow. "What...what happened?"

Alanda said, "You mean...here? Them? Or...."

"No," Marion said. "I remember the earthquake this morning and the tsunami."

"That was three days ago, Marion," Alanda told her.

"What?" Marion could not manage the thought or the timeline in her addled brain.

"They think you have a concussion," Alanda said. "But there are no CTIs or MRIs or even X-rays. The real hospital was demolished. So you have to stay in bed here until you feel better. When they're sure you're okay to walk around and...." Alanda tensed up. "Maybe get out of here."

Marion now noticed the IV in her arm and the glucose bottle feeding her. "Is the water gone? From the tsunami?"

"Mostly. I guess all of it, yeah. Just puddles."

"That's good," Marion allowed.

The two women sat in silence as the sounds of pain and suffering rolled over them. Then Marion remembered, "Dan." She turned her foggy attention to Alanda—who shook her head no. "What?" Marion said. "What do you mean?"

Alanda teared up instantly. "They aren't here."

"They?"

"Lucas and Dan."

"What…what do you mean?" Marion repeated because she had nothing else.

"I've looked everywhere," Alanda said. "Checked every tent and manifest. They're not here."

Marion assumed the worst. "Are they…?"

"I don't know," Alanda said honestly, her tears increasing. "They're not on the dead list, at least."

Marion tried to sit up, but the throbbing in her head dropped her back down. After a moment to let the pain subside, she said, "So where are they?"

"There are a lot of people still missing," Alanda said—then added hopefully, "They'll turn up. I know it. I can feel it. Lucas is still alive. I just…I know it."

Her increased sobbing did not align with her stated hopes.

Marion chose to be positive—more for Alanda than herself. "They're fine, I'm sure. With all this craziness, it could be almost impossible to locate someone. I'm sure they're looking for us, and we'll all be reunited before too long." She took Alanda's hand. "Hang in there. As soon as I'm up, there'll be two of us to look. Okay?"

As Alanda gave a less-than-assured nod, a Black soldier approached. Appearing to be about Alanda's age, he wore a flak-jacket, helmet—fully armed. He asked simply, "Americans?"

Marion said, "Yes. And you are?"

"Sgt. Ashton Mosley, ma'ams. I'm from Oakland, California, and I'm gonna make sure you get out of this shithole okay. Okay?"

Marion said, "Our husbands are—"

Mosley said, "Husbands. Plural? You both have husbands?"

Alanda nodded, then said, They were taken."

"Taken?" Mosely said. "By who?"

"Soldiers," Alanda told him. "Local soldiers. In a different truck."

Marion said, "Are you sure?"

"Well, I think," Alanda said with uncertainty.

"I see," Sgt. Mosely said, nodding—possibly thinking of some alternative theories. "Well, there was a lot of confusion that day. Lots of folks got separated from their loved ones. But we're doing our best to reunite everyone. Mostly having success. I'll walk you through the process, and we'll see what we can turn up. All right?"

Again, Alanda nodded blankly.

Marion said, "They may have gone with a woman—Lana something—who worked for the cardboard company."

"ARC?" he said. "That's probably good. They take care of their people."

Marion said, "What do you mean 'probably'?"

Mosely hesitated, then said, "I shouldn't have said that—put it that way. Uh, let's just, uh, I'll see what I can find out. It's probably fine." This time he caught himself. "Sorry. I just...." He seemed flummoxed. "Don't mind me. This whole thing is FUBAR."

Marion said, "That's an understatement if ever I heard

one."

Mosely tried to ease their concerns. "Most of them, the ARC people — employees, I guess — are being cared for up at their warehouse. We'll look there first." Then, noting Marion's condition. "Or I can check for you — until you feel better."

He seemed to be asking after her condition, so Alanda told him, "She got a concussion and just woke up, but the doctors said as soon as she did wake up, they would try to come around and check her and, I guess, give her the okay get up."

"I'll check on that as well," Mosely said.

Alanda looked up at him and asked, "Why?"

"Uh," he said, chuckling. "'Cause I've been assigned to this tent, and I guess you're my wards, now." He smiled wide.

Marion said, "That's nice."

If she felt some comfort from his presence, Alanda did not. "Can you find them today?"

"I don't know about that, ma'am, but I can sure look and get back to you."

"His name is Lucas," she said.

"Let me write that down," Mosely said, pulling out a small pad and pen.

Marion could see that many names had been written — some crossed out. Not wanting to know if that meant they were found alive or dead, she said, "Dan Cooper. Daniel Robert Cooper."

As Sgt. Mosely wrote that down, he asked Alanda, "And you, ma'am."

"Lucas David Tucker, the Third."

"The Third," Mosely said with a smile.

"He's White," Alanda said. "I'm Alanda."

"Okay," Mosely said, making notes. "Age?"

"Twenty-six," she said.

"That's my age," Mosely said, smiling.

Alanda nodded and looked away.

Marion said, "Dan is forty-six. He'll be forty-seven next month. I'm Marion."

"Okay," Mosely said. "That all can help."

"Do you need physical descriptions?" Marion asked.

"No. Ya'll, White folks all look alike."

Marion snapped a look — but found young Mosely smiling. He said, "Sorry. Just a joke."

Alanda was not laughing either.

Poor Sgt. Ashton Mosely stood still, obviously unsure of what to do next. He finally went with, "Okay, then. I'll see what I can find and report back to you." Then he tried another small joke. "Don't go anywhere!"

Marion snapped another of those looks to find Mosely smiling even wider. Giving him the benefit of the doubt, she said, "I won't. For now."

"Fair enough," he said. Then, with a final nod of his head and a "Ma'ams," he left.

After a moment, Alanda said, "Do you think he'll find them?"

"I hope so," Marion said.

But hope did not infuse her words.

7

After two more days and no word from anyone other than a harried doctor giving a tentative okay, Marion was up from her cot, walking — if shakily — out of the tent.

What she saw made her gasp.

A colony of tents had been erected — some with red crosses, some with red half-moons, some with no markings, some olive drab with American flags, some not. They covered a large open field that had been a park the week before.

No doubt chosen for its altitude — at least a hundred feet above the ocean — one could have imagined the spot as a pleasant sightseeing spot if not for the steady stream of covered bodies being shuffled away.

"Oh my god," Marion said.

"I know, right?" Alanda said. "It's been like this for five days. Day in, day out. The injured are brought in from God knows where, and the dead are taken away to…."

She could not finish.

As they walked between two of the large tents toward the lip of the site, the ground shook slightly. Marion reflexively reached for something to steady herself, but her hand found nothing.

Alanda saw and took her hand, saying, "Aftershock. I swear there have been thousands — like every half-hour. I am so sick of the ground swaying I can't stand it."

"It was a big quake," Marion said of the initial temblor as she regained her verticality and forged ahead. When they had a clear view, she gasped again.

The remnants of their host city looked like the aftermath of war. The water had receded fully, leaving debris in every nook and cranny, small and large — cars and boats, furniture and appliances — an airplane.

"My god," Marion said again. "How did anyone survive that."

Alanda said, "Most didn't. We were lucky. When I see that Lana chick, I am going to hug her until she explodes. If she hadn't —"

"Hopefully, she made it out," Marion said, tersely.

Alanda said nothing further about the mysterious woman who saved them.

A voice behind them said, "Ah, ladies. I found you."

Both women turned to find their guardian sergeant Ashton Mosely, still in full combat-regalia, ordnance hanging from every part of his uniform.

Alanda proved the terse one this time. "I thought you were coming right back."

"Well, I wanted to," the young man said, "but my CO had other plans for me. I've been running my ass off all over this shithole and back."

He heard himself after the fact. "Sorry, ma'am." He looked at Marion, then turned to Alanda. "Ma'ams."

Alanda moved past his vocabulary issues. "Did you find him? Lucas?"

Mosely looked at her, then Marion, then back to Alanda. "Maybe," he said with great caution. "There's not much in the way of, uh, funeral services and what not. The rough count is maybe 100,000 dead, most from the, um, whatever it was. Maybe more."

Marion said, "You mean the earthquake and the tsunami."

Mosely hesitated. "If that's what it was."

Marion's eyes narrowed the way they did when she woke up at three in the morning to find Dan packing, saying, "I have to catch a 4:30. I'll be back in a week. Two, tops." Marion Cooper had come to loath the international hardware business.

Copper.

She said, "What are you saying, Sergeant?" Hoping the official appellative would prod him to an honest reply.

The young soldier looked around — as if to make sure they were alone — then back. But he did not say anything.

So Alanda added, "I don't understand. It wasn't a tidal wave? An earthquake?" Her unspoken sentiment was all but audible. *What could it have been if it wasn't one of those?* Wasn't everyone in agreement that that was exactly what had happened?

What else could kill a hundred thousand or more?

Mosely checked for their privacy again, then said quietly, "There's chatter that, um…maybe it was an attack."

"An *attack*?" Alanda blurted.

Marion said, "Honey," and touched Alanda's arm, encouraging her to respect the soldier's attempt at honesty. Then she asked him, "Would it have been part of that…war we heard about?"

"Oh," he said. "You heard about it, huh?" He considered

this a moment, then asked, "May I inquire as to how? From who?"

"That woman…we mentioned."

"Jana?" he said.

"Lana," Alanda said.

"Right," he said — then went silent again.

Marion became impatient. "So? Was it?"

Mosely looked around again, shuffled his feet, adjusted his weapon. "I can't really say for sure, ma'am. That or maybe something else. We're not supposed to talk about it. Direct orders. 'Sowing chaos,' you know. The usual." He chuckled nervously.

Marion tried to read between his obfuscations. "But there are rumors that…the…."

When she could not organize the myriad clashing thoughts in her head, Marion Cooper went with restating the not-so-obvious, "You're saying the earthquake and tsunami that we felt and *saw*…didn't happen? It was…an act of *war*? Is that what you're saying, Sergeant?"

Young Mosely scanned around one more time as he said, "I'm sorry, ma'am. I really can't." He turned and stepped back a bit to allow them to pass. "This way, please."

Marion gave him another glare — the kind usually reserved for Dan — and started ahead. Alanda gave Ashton Mosely a long, intense look — one that said, *You and I, people of color, get lied to all the time by White people. Are you going to clutch your blackness and tell me what's going on or be a pawn of them?*

All of that with one look. Ashton Mosely read it perfectly. He looked away. "After you, ma'am." Now he got the Marion glare from Alanda as well. But at least she went.

When they were back in the central "square" in the middle of the tent city, Marion stopped, causing the others to stop with her.

"Where are we going, Sergeant?" she said.

Mosely took a breath. "Well, ma'am. When we can't find a survivor, we, um...." He looked askance. "We, uh...."

"Yes?" Marion said. "Check the morgue? What?"

"Sort of, ma'am, but, um...."

"For fuck's sake, Sergeant. Just say it. The dead. Where's the tent? Are we going there now?"

Alanda choked back tears with a gulping stutter.

Mosely steeled himself. "What we tell people, ma'am, is that it's nothing like anything you ever imagined. It's worse, times ten. Not a tent. Times a hundred or a thousand. I'm just...." He sounded like he was choking up as well. "I'm just trying to prepare you, is all, ma'am."

Marion said, "I'm prepared. Let's go."

No amount of preparation could have primed her for what came next.

8

The four-field soccer practice complex was huge. Vast. And the bodies stretched out as far as they could see. Some piled three deep.

"Oh...my...God," Alanda said, and fell to her knees, unable to breathe.

"Let me help you, ma'am," Mosely said, reaching down. But she was not ready to stand and waved him off. Mosely looked to Marion, who had paled. "I tried to warn you, ma'am."

"I understand, Sergeant," Marion said, thinking that no one *could* prepare anyone for what she was seeing.

She had no words. Nothing. Her mind filled only with the awfulness of what stretched out before her as Alanda unsteadily rose to her feet with Ashton Mosely's help.

"Oh my God, above," she said through flowing tears. Then it hit her. "You don't expect us to go looking for...for Lucas in...in *there*?"

"It's the only way, ma'am," Mosely said. "You don't have to. No one *has* to. There are no rules or anything. No laws." Then he scoffed. "There are no damn laws anywhere around here."

Marion passed on the urge to challenge his notion.

Mosely told Alanda, "You can just go on home if you like, ma'am, and when we locate him…." He considered his words carefully. "Whatever his condition…we will let you know by phone or email or snail mail, whatever you prefer. You can register—"

"Enough!" Marion all but shouted, never looking away from the awful sights before her—bodies laid out in neat rows, hundreds of rows with….

"How many?" she said.

"I think I heard ten-to twelve-thousand, ma'am. It's down a bit."

"Jesus," Marion said, seeing the grieving mothers, fathers, brothers and sisters, extended families, and neighbors—the wailing, the screaming, the pointless prayers after the fact.

The horror.

And even worse, at the far side, bulldozers shoving bodies into a mass grave, a trench that ran hundreds of feet.

Without taking her eyes away, Marion said, "Are those the ones no one could identify?"

Mosely said, "Ma'am, those are the ones no one could identify as *human*. Faces gone. Teeth, hands, feet, other…body parts."

Alanda looked like she might faint again and began mumbling her go-to oath—words only she knew—under her breath.

Marion said, "What do you mean, Sergeant?"

Mosely said, "It was like…I was with a buddy the first day, and he looked down and laughed. He said, 'Hey, lookit this, looks like my wife's favorite dildo.'"

Marion threw him a look.

He said, "I'm sorry, uh, sex toy."

Marion shook her head and looked away. But Mosely was not done.

He said, "Anyway, he picked it up, kinda laughing and...."

The women blanched. Alanda closed her eyes.

The young sergeant said, softer, "'Yeah,' my other buddy says. 'Only, Arthur, that's no dildo. It's the real thing.' A penis, ma'ams. Chopped off and cauterized...erect like that, and just left there on the ground. We've found...breasts like that, and just...all kinds of weird shit and—"

Marion said, "Stop. That's more than enough detail, Sergeant."

"Sorry, ma'am," Mosely said. "Ma'ams."

Marion said, repulsed, "Who would *do* that?"

"Who or *what*?" Ashton Mosely said.

This time when Marion showed him an intense stare, she focused on understanding the unthinkable. "What are you saying *now*?"

"I don't know what I'm saying, ma'am. I've heard chatter, like I said. None of it makes any sense. But in that big tent over there, on the right, it's *filled* with body parts—all kinds of body parts—men, women, kids—none of them going together, or any way to figure out which part goes with which body. It's freakin' weird, I'll tell you. Somebody or something was up to some freaky, horrible shit, is all I know." He went wan. "I went in there. Once. That was all it took. I couldn't eat for two days. I've never.... And in this heat? Shit. Another day and there won't be anything but goo."

Marion had seen and heard enough. "Let's go." She turned to leave.

Alanda stopped her. "We're not even going to look? What

if Lucas is out there?"

"It doesn't matter."

"But what if he's alive?"

"Then he won't be here."

Alanda looked as if her whole world had just caught fire, burned before her, and left only bitter ashes in her mouth.

Seeing her pain, Marion took another look at the field of death and asked Ashton, "They can't have found everyone yet."

More rhetorical than an actual question—limp hope.

Mosely said, "No, ma'am, I don't believe they ever will. There were bodies washed five or ten miles inland. Some got into rivers, some were eaten by crocs. Some are hung in trees, washed into holes in the ground, caves—some washed back out to sea."

Ashton Mosely sounded haunted by the images already—and the images that would follow. "They may wash back in someday, but who's to say what they're gonna look like at that point. If we could even tell who or what they were. Rotted, half-eaten by sharks, and—"

"Jesus-fucking-Christ, shut up! Stop it!" Alanda shouted, her eyes wide, her face red, her tears on pause for the moment.

Ashton hung his head in shame. "I'm sorry, ma'am. I was just...." He could not find the words to express his own fears, his exasperated confusion and lack of answers.

Marion said, "What, Ashton? What was your point?"

"That earthquakes don't do that, ma'am. What I was talking about before. Not that kind of thing. People do that. Bad people. Or...something else. I don't know."

Marion's intensity did not waver. She understood—if Alanda did not. "'Something'?" Alanda said. "What something? Are you saying *animals*?"

Marion said, "He's saying.... The rumors of there being a

war, an attack, has some credence—if you find things like that. Horrors like that."

"The war's not a rumor, ma'am, Mosely said. "It's real. It's happening. It's just…what *kind* of war. That's the question."

Alanda did not find solace in his indirect answers. "What does that *mean*? I don't understand. Where is Lucas? Is he here? Is he dead? Was he killed by soldiers in this…war? What are you *saying*?!" She was yelling again.

Ashton said, "I'm saying I don't know, ma'am. About anything. But as regards your husband, the only way to know for sure is to go out there and check toe-tags—if they have 'em—look at the faces, maybe some scar or mole or something you might remember that will help you identify your loved one. A tattoo."

"Lucas didn't like tattoos."

"I understand, ma'am. I'm just saying the only way to know for sure that he's not out there is to go and look. I'm sorry, but that's the best we can do—and there's no guarantee of *that*."

"I get that, Ashton," Alanda said, curtly. "I get that part, okay? What I don't get is why you are telling us that someone is…cutting off peoples' *genitals*, for Chrissake! What does that *mean*?"

"I don't know, Ms. Tucker," Ashton said. "I'm very sorry that I mentioned it. It was stupid. I apologize."

Alanda looked out into the field, and her tearful shudders returned. She made her decision. "I can't go out there. That's not happening."

Marion patted her, met Ashton's concerned gaze, looked out across the awfulness and said, "I'll go."

Alanda looked up. "No."

"Yes," Marion said. "I need to know. Who am I kidding? I can't leave this place without at least looking for Dan. I'll look for Lucas too. Okay?"

Alanda sort of nodded — sort of didn't.

Marion asked Mosely, "Is there someplace I should start?"

"The 'European' section, I guess. It's marked," he said. "That's where they put all the White people. All the rest are kind of…all mixed up together."

"I'm sorry," Marion heard herself say, speaking on behalf of non-complicit Caucasians, living *or* dead.

Mosely nodded, seeming to understand, and said, "I'll show you where it is."

"Okay," Marion said. "Are there masks or anything?"

"Over there," Ashton said, pointing at a *welcome* station.

Then he turned to Alanda and asked if she would be okay, left here alone. She nodded weakly, so young Sergeant Ashton Mosely walked Marion over to sign in, get a mask, and be read the rules.

Not a dozen bodies into the first row, Marion was crying — seeing the death masks for the horror they were, some frozen with their final fears, caught unprepared for that finality. Bodies bloated and black, battered and torn, rotting in the sun.

It was all Marion could do to keep from vomiting. Had she eaten anything that day, it would have come up.

She stopped, stared down what seemed an endless row of decomposing bodies and felt her soul collapse inside her. "Let's…." she said. "Can we…."

"Yes, ma'am," Sgt. Mosely said. "The European section is over here." And he led the way through the rows and rows of people of color.

The exclusive Whites-only section was no happier a place. In some ways, it felt worse — Marion seeing people she might have known back home, in town, in church. Back when she went to church — before she realized the pointlessness and hypocrisy. Long before she saw four soccer fields full of something no god could allow. All ages and builds, men and women — and so many children. Babies.

Again, Marion stopped — feeling faint.

Ashton said, "Maybe if you concentrated on men their age, ma'am. Their build, you know."

Marion gave a rapid nod and tried not to breathe.

9

They found Alanda sitting on a bench just outside the soccer complex, staring into the ghost-filled space in front of her—either imagining the worst or trying not to.

"Hey," Marion said, struggling to sound supportive, if not positive. "You okay?"

"Huh?" Alanda said, looking up. She had apparently not heard them approach, had not seen them standing almost in front of her. "No," she told them. "Did you...."

She could not bring herself to even ask the question.

Marion sat beside her on the bench. "No. And that's a good thing," she said.

Alanda said, "He might still be alive."

"I'm sure he is," Marion lied. Then, feeling bad about that because she had been raised to tell the truth, said, "I hope he is."

"Your Dan, too," Alanda said.

"Dan, too."

The ground shook slightly. Everyone got still and waited. Then it was over.

Ashton Mosely shifted on his heels. He said, "Ma'ams, I

probably need to check in. I can take you back now. I see a jeep over there. Maybe we can get a ride."

"That would be good," Marion said. "I'm still not fully recovered, I think. My legs. I'm a bit shaky."

"Here you go," he said, offering her a hand up. Then Alanda. "Ma'am."

Alanda took his hand as Marion had, accepting his help. But rather than let go of his hand, of him, of another human being who cared, she clutched tighter and looked into his eyes, her own eyes fraught with fear and loss — fear of loss — and she said, "It will be okay, won't it?"

Mosely looked uncomfortable for a moment, then he said, "I'm afraid I can't promise that, ma'am. I'd like to, but…."

Alanda…relaxed. She said, still looking the young Black soldier in the eye, "Thank you for being honest." He nodded and did his best to smile, but it wasn't much.

Marion took his other arm to steady herself, and the three of them walked to the jeep. Mosely asked the driver, "Can we get a ride to the American hotel?"

"Sure, hop in," the kid from Omaha said. And added, as they climbed into the 4x4, "Hot as hell in all this gear, ain't it? I'm hatin' this shit."

"At least you're alive," Alanda said.

"Just drive, Corporal," Mosely said, pulling rank. "Keep your thoughts to yourself."

"Yes, Sergeant," the kid said, and did.

———————

After a twenty-minute ride that felt like two hours — waiting for opposing truck traffic on single lanes where half the road was gone; homeless families walking the shoulders, headed inland, probably to relatives' homes; a helicopter rescue of a child found alive in his family's crashed car at the bottom of a ravine — Nebraska, as Ashton called their driver, stopped on the backside of the first mountain in the busy parking lot of one of the last remaining hotels.

"Door to door service, ladies," he said. "Hotel USA."

"Thank you," both Alanda and Marion told him as Mosely helped them down to the ground, saying, "Hang on for me, Nebraska. I need a hitch back to C&C."

"You got it, bro'," the kid said.

Ashton ignored him.

A bus was taking on passengers — many of them bandaged — while the occasional military truck drove others away. Some meandered, still looking dazed.

Alanda asked, "Where are they going?"

"Home, ma'am," he said.

"I want to go home," Alanda said. Then added, "I think."

Marion patted her and told their shepherd, "Thank you, Sergeant."

"Ashton, ma'am," he said, and pulled two cards from his pocket.

He said to Alanda. "If you need anything, anything at all...." Then realizing where his gaze had lingered, said to Marion, "You too, ma'am, Ms. Cooper." And he spoke to them both. "I'm here for you." He looked around vaguely and added, "Well, somewhere."

He smiled, and Marion returned it — Alanda still too shell-shocked to hear humor.

Ashton Mosely said, "I'm not exactly assigned to you, but it kind of works that way. So just call if you need help or answers — if we have any — and we'll get back to you."

He handed the card to Marion since Alanda continued

to watch the wandering wounded. "Alanda?" he said, and she turned to him. "This is our company card," he said. "If you need anything."

Alanda nodded and took the card without reading it.

Ashton said, "My cell number's on the back, and it usually works here. Reception around the city is still pretty good. 'The towers didn't topple,' as my CO says. So, you know, call me direct if you need...well, whatever. I'll try to get right to you as soon as I can."

Alanda came out of her trance to ask, "Are you leaving us here alone now?"

Marion said, "We'll be fine, dear. This is a hotel for Americans. They can help us sort things out and...figure out what we're going to do next. Right, Sergeant?"

"Yes, ma'am," he said

"I want to go home," Alanda said again.

"We will," Marion assured her. "As soon as we can. Okay?"

Alanda's piteous look turned rancid. "Lucas is dead. It's not okay. Okay?"

Marion ignored the sarcasm, knowing it was a reaction to circumstance, and told Ashton, "We'll call if we need you. Otherwise, jeez, good luck with all this."

"I'm gonna need it," the young soldier said with a surrendered chuckle. Then he turned to Alanda. "It won't be much longer. They're getting people out pretty fast, now."

Alanda offered a sallow grin and nod, then went back to watching the departing people as a stiff Captain walked up to Mosely and said, "Sergeant, are you done here?"

"Yessir, I believe so."

"Then get this vehicle moving. They're more waiting to

get in."

Everyone looked but did not see any other vehicles. Still, Mosely said, "Yessir. Right away, sir."

With a last nod to Marion and what might have passed for a longing look at Alanda—as if he knew he would never see her again and would regret that—Aston Mosely jogged the short distance to the jeep, hopped in and said, "Back to C&C, Nebraska. Captain's orders."

The last two words sounded as sarcastic as Alanda's words moments before. The White kid grinned, ground the jeep into gear, and lunged away.

Ashton Mosely never took his eyes off Alanda.

The Captain said, "Ladies," nodded officially, and walked away.

Marion knew not to take male military servitude seriously, but she did watch the straight-backed officer until he was out of sight, noticing that the entire time, he looked up at the sky, this way and that, as if expecting something to appear.

10

The night trudged long, hot, and uncomfortable Alanda and Marion were forced to share a bed — and a room with an elderly couple from Missoula. The man snored. His wife kept nudging him, going so far as to physically roll him over once, but he grumbled in his sleep and rolled back onto his back to saw logs at the ceiling the rest of the night.

Marion thought she might have gotten an hour's rest, cumulatively — if that. Fortunately, Alanda conked out the moment her head hit the pillow, and she did not stir an inch until morning — still as the dead lying in the soccer fields.

At least one of them might have enough clarity to navigate the next day.

As it turned out, they got summoned to the front desk to be told — quietly — that airline arrangements had been made for them to fly out in the early evening. They were free to "enjoy" their day in the meantime.

Marion might have had a snide remark for the concierge, but a couple from Alabama had heard and demanded to know how "you two got a goddam ticket out when we didn't!" They had been at the hotel a day longer.

Feeling renewed and surprisingly feisty, Alanda told them to, "Fuck off."

The man became more enraged. "Don't talk to my wife like that, you little Black bitch!"

It took Marion and two busboys to pull Alanda off the man. They were given their tickets and asked to leave—and not return.

"Happily," Marion said.

On their way out, she told Alanda, "That was impressive."

"Cracker asshole," was all Alanda had left for the shithead.

Marion laughed and flagged down an American in a passing jeep. "Hey! Nebraska!"

The kid stopped and gave them a ride to find Sgt. Mosely for a knowing thank-you and final goodbye.

The desert-tan camo Command-and-Control tent—apparently the green jungle-issue tents were being used elsewhere—bustled inside, dozens of satellite computers and phones in use by a cadre of intelligence officers and their non-coms. Americans had been joined by Australian and French service personnel as well—the former because of their proximity, the latter because the country had once been under French rule, and France still maintained a naval base on an outlying island.

Large maps, topos, and drone photos hung all around the inside walls of the high tent—for most of the country, north and south, it appeared, with a clear demarcation of the two—tables strewn with photos of destruction and gore.

At one of those tables, Ashton was idly flipping through some of those photographs when he looked up to find Marion and Alanda having just entered the tent. A young PFC pointed to Ashton, who met them halfway.

"You got a plane out, I hear," Mosely said.

"And you no doubt had something to do with that," Marion said with a teacher's *disapproving* smile.

"Not supposed to," he said, meeting her grin.

Alanda, more centered today, said, "Well, I don't care who did what. I'm just glad to be leaving this awful place. I couldn't have stood another day here."

"I figured," Ashton said.

Marion said, "I offered to stay and help, but the government—"

"Is in complete disorder," Ashton said, all but scowling. "I'll walk you to your bus," he said with what Marion read as a somewhat paranoid glance around. Mosely added, "It's probably best you wait at the airport. It's pretty crazy here."

He was right. The staging area outside turned out to be even busier than when the women arrived just minutes before. Trucks, jeeps, Humvees, and buses all jockeying for a space as travelers eager to leave hopped out of one to be herded into another. Others walked around still in a daze awaiting guidance— or direct orders—on what to do next.

"Uh, this way," Ashton said, pointing off to the side.

Alanda stopped, confused. "But the buses are—"

"Just for a minute," Ashton told her—and gently took her elbow in his hand.

Alanda looked down at his hand on her flesh and said, "Okay."

When Marion did not object, the handsome young soldier led the women to a private spot between two tents. When he stopped, Marion asked, "What's up, Sergeant?"

Nervously checking around, Ashton said, "I shouldn't be telling you this—"

"Then don't," Marion said. When he looked at her oddly, not understanding, she said, "You don't need to get in trouble. All of this is enough, I'm sure."

Getting them out early.

"Thank you, ma'am," he said. "But it's not that. You see, we...."

Alanda's hopes rose. "Did you find him? Did you find Lucas?" Then her fears took over. "Oh no. Is he...." She started to say dead, then went with silence.

Ashton stammered. "Um, no, ma'am. I mean, yes. I mean...." He took a breath. "We have received no word on that situation, yet. I'm sorry."

He turned to Marion. "On *them*."

He nervously checked around again as Marion asked with stern impatience. "What is it you feel you need to tell us, Sergeant. Just say it."

Mosely looked back a beat, then said, "It's just you might start...hearing things."

Alanda asked, "What kinds of things?"

"Weird things," he said.

"Such as?" Marion said.

"Well, look, nothing's confirmed, but—"

Now Alanda turned stern. "Ashton, just *say* it."

He *said,* "That's the first time you've called me Ashton."

That sentiment behind that notion disturbed her. "I don't think so, but...just tell us what you want to tell us so we can go."

"I understand," he said, regret in his tone.

Marion pushed him. "What kind of weird things, Ashton?"

"Rumors," he said ominously.

"Sergeant, *please,*" Marion said.

Again, Mosely checked around before saying, "It may not

have been an earthquake." He widened his eyes for effect and watched carefully for their response.

Marion said, "What else could it have been?"

Alanda threw in, "Yeah, we saw it. Heard it. Felt it. It was...fucking terrible."

"I know, I know," Mosely said quickly.

"So?" Marion prodded him.

The young soldier kept dancing around the issue that he had raised. But he managed to say, "I misspoke. It was an earthquake...sort of."

Exasperated, Marion rolled her eyes and threw her hands out. "Ashton."

He bucked up. "It's what *caused* the earthquake, ma'am."

Alanda said, "What do you mean?"

Marion said, "You're saying it wasn't—"

"Nature," the sergeant cut it. "At least not any nature we know." He looked up to the heavens with suspicion and concern.

Marion read the look first. "Are you saying...wait...*aliens*? That some...." She could not even finish such a preposterous theorem.

Ashton *nodded*.

Alanda looked at Marion then back to Mosely. "Are you fucking with us?"

"No!" Ashton said. "I wouldn't do that! I shouldn't even be telling you this."

"Then why are you?" Marion demanded. And added, "It's ludicrous."

"I know, ma'am," he said. "But apparently, there's... evidence."

"What kind of evidence?" Marion said. "Hearsay? Rumors, like you said."

"No, ma'am. Visual evidence," he said. "We've heard there might be some...pictures out there. Some people may have taken pictures with their cellphones. Videos."

"And have they come forward?"

"No, ma'am. They've been taken away."

"Taken by whom?"

"We don't know, ma'am. But they're gone." He parsed his words carefully. "Like your husbands, ma'ams. They're gone. Anybody who may have seen something seems to be missing. Taken away."

"By aliens," Alanda said, trying to grasp the notion and failing totally.

Marion was not buying it, "You're saying that Dan and Lucas were abducted by aliens."

"Possibly, ma'am, yes."

Marion stewed. "That is the most patently ridiculous thing I've ever heard in my life. Are you kidding me? Is this the best our military can come up with when they can't find victims of a natural disaster?" She turned away, shaking her head. "Aliens. Jesus."

"Well, the thing is, ma'am...." Mosely breathed out heavily. "I should not be telling you this."

Marion turned back. "You keep saying that. But hey, you're this far deep into it. You might as well speak your piece."

Ashton looked embarrassed, but he went for it. "The thinking is that—the possible theory—is that this whole thing may have been an act of war."

"*War of the Worlds*?" Marion said, sarcastically.

"That's been mentioned. Something like that. Yes, ma'am."

Alanda said, "I thought it was an earthquake."

"Right," Ashton nodded, getting warmed up, his

enthusiasm returning. "That's what it looked like."

"But it wasn't?" Alanda seemed to be having trouble wrapping her head around the concept. She had a recent MBA—a degree that did not fully prepare her for either natural or unnatural science.

Ashton Mosely was wound up. "Yeah," he said. "Like they have some...secret weapon or something. Like a...beam, they can aim at the earth and cause earthquakes and landslides and shit. Floods, whatever. That tsunami."

Marion said flatly. "The aliens."

Ashton said, "No, ma'am, the North. They've been threatening for over a year and—I'm sure you read the State Department warnings about travel there."

"It didn't say anything about aliens or secret beams."

"No. It wouldn't," Mosely said. "I mean, think about it." He nodded to himself. "And to be fair, they might not have known. They probably didn't. Who could? I mean, look at this crazy shit. What happened. It's off the charts. What *else* could have caused it?"

He appeared baffled—and scared.

Marion was done. She said, "Alanda, our bus is waiting."

She gently put her hand around Alanda's wrist and started backing away, her eyes never leaving the wide-eyed young soldier.

"I swear, ma'am," Mosely said. "I'm not making this up. Swear to God. We're on High Alert. Satellites are being rerouted to cover the area 24/7. We have AWACs planes coming in today. Or they're already here. We have spotters out in the field. On ships and...." He nodded behind them. "...up in the mountains. I've never seen anything like it. And I was deployed to Afghanistan, my first tour. It's crazier than shit, I know. But I swear, I am not making this up."

Marion continued backing away.

"Shit," Mosely said. "I knew I shouldn't have told you."

"That, I would agree with," Marion said.

"I just wanted you to know," he said. "In case you hear things. I didn't want you to worry."

"Oh, I'm worried, all right," Marion said. "But not about aliens."

Alanda stopped and retrieved her wrist. "But what if he's right? What if he's telling the truth?" She looked at the now abashed soldier and asked, "Are you telling us the truth, Ashton?"

That worked on him better than torture ever could. "On my mother's life. I swear to God," he said, looking her straight in the eye.

Over it, Marion said, "Well, for her case and yours, I hope He's listening."

With that, she took Alanda's hand and forcefully led her away. "We don't want to miss our bus."

Alanda went, but she looked back with confusion, concern, and sympathy — Ashton returning it all. Then she turned away — and he saw two officers coming his way.

Time to go.

As Marion tried to figure out which bus was theirs, she said, "That boy has lost his mind."

But Alanda was feeling kind — and confused. "What if it's true?"

"He's insane."

"How do you know that for sure?"

Marion stopped, gathered her thoughts, and said, "Alanda, honey, we just met the other day, so I don't really know you or your husband — *Lucas* — but I will promise you this, that young man, that soldier, is *way* out of line and probably well out of his mind."

"But why would he make up something like that?"

Marion said, "Look around you. Have you ever seen anything this horrible? Could you ever have imagined anything this awful in your life? And look at these people — the survivors. Vacant eyes and souls — like zombies. The almost-dead, walking and wondering what the hell might happen next. Scared out of their damn minds. Like us."

When Alanda did not interrupt, Marion said, "In a situation like this, we tell ourselves anything to get past it. To survive."

Alanda started to cry. "But what if…." She could not finish.

Marion advised her, "Forget that conversation. If Lucas is alive, he will be found, and he will come home to you."

As Alanda shook from fear and tears, Marion took her by her elbows and looked directly into her reddened face. "If not — and you need to accept this — if he is not alive, he will not be coming home. That's the reality, and you understand that. I know you do. I'm sorry."

Marion chose her next words carefully. "There was an earthquake, a powerful, awful earthquake, that caused a tsunami that destroyed this town and others around it and took, apparently, over a hundred thousand human lives. A *natural disaster*. An earthquake and a tidal wave. Not invisible war beams or aliens."

She gave Alanda a last tight squeeze for comfort, then looked up toward the mountains. "I hope Dan is out there somewhere, trying to get back to me. He's all I had in the world, but…."

She could not finish, the pain overwhelming.

When she looked back to her young companion—her ward—Marion's eyes were just as red, just as tear-streaked. She said, "But when he comes back to me, *if* he comes back to me, it won't be from outer space."

Alanda said, "But where did their truck go? Why didn't it go where *we* did? Where did they take them? And what happened to them? I want to know! Goddammit! I want to know! Why am I alive, and he's *not*? You tell me that, Marion! Tell me!"

Alanda's shouts drew the attention of camo'd Phnongtuk soldiers with guns.

Marion saw them starting over and said. "Alanda, we were lucky, is all. We survived. A lot of people didn't."

Alanda persisted. "But why? What if it *was* aliens? How do we know it *wasn't*! They're out there. They have to be. It's a big universe. Why wouldn't they come here and…and see how shitty we all are to each other…why *wouldn't* they want to take us over? Conquer us. *Kill* us. Just to make the universe a better place?"

Realizing Alanda was lost to loss, Marion returned to her soothing countenance. Her mom voice. "Believe whatever you want, dear. Whatever helps. But I will tell you this, I walked through that field of bodies and body parts." Her voice dropped, laced with anger and surrender. "In a way, I'm glad I did. Because what I saw was the work of God. A cruel, heartless God. Not man, not aliens, not war. Just an angry God. Maybe angry because of what you said—that we aren't worth keeping. So he just decided, 'To hell with them. I am going to wipe out a hundred thousand of these ungrateful, warring, awful examples of human waste.' Maybe that *is* it. I don't know. If you want to believe it was something else, go ahead. But know this, someday, this will be over for you. Someday, you will move on. You won't ever forget it, but you *will* move on — with or without Lucas. You will survive this. In the meantime, I will pray for you."

Alanda said, "To who? Your God that hates us?"

"He's all I've got," Marion said, and turned to locate their bus.

Alanda blew up. "That's not good enough, Marion, goddammit! I want to know where he is! I WANT TO KNOW WHAT THE HELL HAPPENED TO MY FUCKING HUSBAND, GODDAMMIT!"

Marion remained moved. "I think this is our bus," she said, having found a ragged piece of cardboard in the window that read, "Aerport."

"No!" Alanda screamed. Marion looked — then turned away.

Got on the bus.

She did not see the two local armed soldiers accost Alanda. They spoke in perfect English, "Get on the bus, Mrs. Tucker. You must get on the bus, now."

"What? How did you…? Let go of me!"

She tried to pull away, but the soldiers held tight and repeated, "You must get on this bus now and leave."

Before Alanda could protest any more, one of them leaned close and said, "Or you must stay."

The meaning — the threat — rang clear. Alanda looked down at their gloved hands, tight around her forearms.

They let go, and somehow that threat was even stronger.

Alanda looked to see the bus door closing. "Wait! Don't go! Wait!" she shouted and ran, pounding on the door — which opened.

Alanda stepped in, the doors closed, and the bus drove

away.

Off to one side, Ashton watched. This time, *his* eyes went red and teary.

The moment broke when his CO came up behind with the latest orders, "We're moving out. SoPac Command says we're done. This place and what happens here is of no more interest to you, Sergeant. Do you understand?"

Ashton Mosely stared several seconds, conflicted. Then he nodded and said, "Yessir. We're pulling out In understand, sir."

"Good," his CO said. "Report to C&C, turn in your gear, and we'll see you back home, son. Dismissed."

Ashton Mosely gave a half-salute, not out of disrespect but loss, and turned away. His CO watched him but had more on his mind that a disturbed sergeant.

He looked up into the sky.

11

Deep in the remote jungled mountains fifty kilometers north of Phnongtuk, nothing seemed to move—no blowing wind, no scurrying animals, no pattering creek. Not even ants. The place felt as desolate as a desert but so densely overgrown as to be impenetrable.

The lone road—more of a lane, grabbed at by every limb and vine surrounding it—ended at a low, cement building with one solid steel door and no windows. The 60'x60' cube had no roof in places but rather tightly-laced rebar providing a pattern of open inches for air—and rain.

In one dark cell of the building, Dan Cooper moaned, naked. His bruised and scabbing knees rested in dank puddles on the cement floor, his arms lashed at the elbows, pulled up and back just short of dislocation, ropes looped through the small spaces between the vine-covered rebar above.

From the otherwise silent corners of this *detainment center*, Dan could hear Lucas's soft crying coming from the next cell over. Though blindfolded, each knew the other was in the same, poor shape.

Lucas said, "Dan? You're still there, right?" He sniffled.

"Yeah, Lucas. That pathetic moaning you hear is me."

"This shit hurts, dude. My arms. I think they're dislocated."

"Probably not. Just feels like it."

"It hurts."

"Yes, it does."

Dan fought the urge to moan more.

"Where are we?" Lucas asked.

"Prison of some sort," Dan said. "Probably in the North."

"Why?"

Dan hesitated. "I'm not sure, Lucas."

"I mean, Why the North? Those soldiers were terrible. Down there. When they took us."

"They were, but...." Dan chose his words carefully. "It's just a guess. I don't know for sure."

Lucas wanted to know, "Why did they bring us here?"

"Probably because we're Americans."

"But they didn't take anyone else, and no one else is here, are they?"

"I don't know. I was knocked unconscious when they brought us. Drugged too, I imagine."

"They put a hood over my head."

"Me too."

"Why would they do that?"

"So we wouldn't know where we were."

"But why?"

Dan sighed again. He needed to figure out how to take care of this kid *and* himself. Plus, "Have you seen that woman Lana who was with us?"

"Why? You think she had us brought here? She had a gun."

"No, Lucas. I was just wondering if you've seen her. I have no further ideas."

Lucas said, "You want me to stop talking."

Dan tried not to feel the many pains in his contorted body with no success. He could only imagine what this sheltered *boy* from Surf City, USA, must be feeling and thinking.

Fearing.

Lucas asked, shakily, "Are they going to kill us?"

Dan had been waiting for that question. He took a deep breath and decided on honesty. "Probably."

"Why?"

"I don't know, Lucas. You'll have to ask them."

Before Lucas could ask anyone anything, Dan heard a loud splash of water, and Lucas cried out. Then he yelled, "Stop it! Stop doing that! Why do you keep doing that!"

Knowing he was next, Dan braced as he heard one of their masked guards screaming in his native tongue at Lucas.

Splashing him again.

Against his better judgement, Dan offered some advice. "Don't antagonize them, Lucas."

"But what do they *want*?!" Lucas yelled as the guard kept screaming at him.

"They want us to stop talking! To stop complaining. They want silence—"

Icy water hit Dan, making his body ache worse than before.

———————

Two days later, guards stomped into Dan Cooper's cell, cut the rope that kept him suspended without removing it from his elbows, then yanked him up, dragged him to another cell, stood him up, chained him to a wall, removed the rope from his arms and the hood from his head.

Blinding light.

Dan squinted for several seconds before he could see his abductors—not that he could make out any more than their dark, soulless eyes peering out from masks in silence.

A tall soldier—tall for these people—who wore a black bandana-like scarf over his face stepped in front of Dan, close, flanked by two masked men with guns trained on Dan's body, generally. Four more masked and armed men stood behind the three in front, guarding the door and their cohort.

Dan took it all in, then said to the man standing in front of him, "You would be my interrogator, I suppose."

The man did not hesitate to punch Dan across the face, throwing his head to one side. Dan knew this was not the time for some clever, pithy Bruce Willis snark. These guys meant business, and smart mouthing would only bring him more pain.

The puncher said, "Why were you in the room?" At least he spoke English.

"What room?" Dan said.

The man punched him again.

Dan said, "Oh, *that* room." One smart-ass line might slide by. But to preclude more abuse, he said, "You mean the woman's apartment."

Regardless of his words or intent, he received another punch—not brutal, not meant to kill or severely injure, just to get his attention.

It worked. Dan said, "We had just met her on the beach, having drinks, on vacation. During the earthquake, she showed up and helped us out of it. To her apartment. That's all."

Another punch—and a warning: "You can either tell the truth about why you were there, what is your business here, or you can die now."

Another punch to enunciate his point.

Dan groaned, said, "Might be better than this."

"You *joke*?" the man yelled — and nodded to his henchmen. Both gun-butted Dan's ribs, causing him to groan deeply and sag.

"Do not lie again," his interrogator told him.

"I'm not lying," Dan said with what little energy he had left for this encounter. "There was the earthquake and the tsunami, and we were cornered, about to drown, and she appeared out of nowhere and led us to her apartment, where it was high and safe. Then your men burst in and — "

"They were not my men," the inquisitor said without emotion.

"Then who were they, and why are we here?"

"Yes. Why are you here?"

"You *brought* us."

"Why are you in our country?"

"I told you my wife and I were on *vacation*."

"No! No vacation! Work!"

Dan shot back. "No! Vacation. With my wife." Then he thought to ask, "Where is my wife?"

"She is gone," the man said.

"Gone?" Dan said. He had thought of every possible outcome for Marion, but hearing that word brought a frightening realization. "Dead? Do you mean she's dead?"

"It doesn't matter," the man said, brushing it off.

"It matters to me," Dan said.

"All that matters to you, 'Dan Cooper,' is what matters to me at this moment. What matters to me is what you are doing in my country. What was your business in my country? That is all that matters to me and those to whom I answer."

Well-spoken for a foreign inquisitor.

Dan shook his head. "I have nothing against you or your people or anything else. I was on vacation with my wife, and there was a terrible earthquake and tidal wave, and I imagine many people are dead, but we were lucky."

"Maybe not so lucky," Black Mask said. "Maybe you are next to die."

Dan said, honestly, "I don't want to die."

"Then answer the question."

"I did," Dan said.

"This time, tell the truth."

"I told the truth."

"WHY ARE YOU HERE!?"

Though Dan knew that shifting tone was part of his interrogator's *technique*—as were the next round of gun butts—he was losing his desire to participate. "I already told you," he said, slumping in pain.

"I will ask you one last time, Why were you in the woman's apartment?"

Dan, beginning to fade, said only, "Earth...quake."

The tall man said, "There was no earthquake."

Dan lifted his head. "What? Then...what was it?" He had seen it—experienced it.

"An act of God," the masked man said. "On our behalf. God fired the first shot of our final, righteous battle for unity."

So, they *were* in the North. Good to know—or not.

After seeing a quarter of what he had seen in his life, Dan was mostly an atheist. Though he calculated his agnosticism might fall on deaf ears, he said, "God doesn't really get involved in wars, you know. He doesn't take sides. Especially for sides that torture innocent people on vacation."

Dan chuckled darkly at his dangerous riposte.

His interrogator appeared visibly insulted. Even behind his black bandana, Dan could see the ire rise instantly. The tall man said, "You would laugh at our God and His intentions?"

Dan held his face as high as he could, looked the evil bastard in the eye, and said, "No. I laugh at your notion that God takes sides in a war — especially a phony one."

Dan saw the man's dark eyes flare a second before the gun butt found its mark on the side of his head this time — and Dan was out.

Bruce Willis would have been proud.

12

Looting had begun in the ravaged town of Phnongtuk. Pillagers smashed windows, stole goods, and set a police station on fire. Remaining aggrieved residents wanted revenge — and food.

The South's leader announced a national emergency and declared martial law, resulting in the shooting of some locals caught breaking the law. Several died, and looting turned to rioting.

Then the ground shook again, nearly as violently as the first time, and the terrified populace ran uphill for their lives, again.

The temblor did not generate a tsunami this time, but the roar equaled the first quake. Only this time, it sounded different as it continued — like jets roaring over, low — as several explosions followed, rocking the small city.

Passengers in planes on the tarmac at the miraculously undamaged airport heard the roars and booms and felt the tremors, evacuees still screaming every time they felt the slightest jolt.

Alanda felt it and tensed but was happy to be on her way

home.

———————

Everything at Dulles International Airport, outside D.C., was calm, relatively speaking. The usual press of suburbanites impatiently passing through long lines to get to their own vacations seemed no worse than any other day. Washingtonians had long learned to wait, if not appreciate that wait, to safeguard against a terrorist blowing them up midair on their way to Cancun or Bruges or Coeur d'Alene.

After twenty-three hours in the air, a relieved but weary Marion stepped out of the jetway to be greeted by six men in black suits and ties.

Sunglasses.

"Ms. Cooper?" one of them said.

"Mrs. Yes."

"Come with us, please."

"Is this about my husband? Did you find Dan?" The hope rang clear in her voice—tinged with fear.

"No, ma'am," the *officer* said. "Just come with us, please."

Marion did not move. "Why? What have I done?"

"Nothing, ma'am," the man behind dark glasses said. "It's for your own safety."

"Why? What…. Why am I not safe?"

"Reporters, ma'am," he said. "Shall we?"

"No, we shan't," Marion Cooper said. "What reporters? What are you talking about?"

"The incident, ma'am."

"You mean the earthquake."

"Yes, ma'am. That and the rest."

"What 'rest'? I don't understand. The tsunami?"

"All of it, ma'am. One of our people will explain in the

car."

"What car?"

"We've arranged safe transportation home for you."

"My sister's picking me up."

"No, ma'am. She was called off."

"Called off? What do you mean? What's going on here?"

As Marion raised her voice, other travelers began to stare.

The agent maintained his motion-free manner. "Ma'am, you are completely safe. We're U.S. Marshals assigned to assist you from your plane to your car, where another agent will debrief you on the ride home."

"Debrief me? On what?"

"Ma'am.... Ms. Cooper—"

"Mrs."

"Yes, I'm sorry. Mrs. Cooper. There's nothing to worry about, I promise you. You are completely safe. You've done nothing wrong."

"Then why do I need six men with guns who are constantly looking around like I'm the friggin' president. Why do I need all of you to get to a car I didn't order?"

The Marshal was done debating. "Ma'am.... Mrs. Cooper... please." He pointed in the direction he wanted her to walk.

With a scowl and a pout, Marion Cooper walked that way.

Nothing on their march seemed unusual—except for the stares of passengers and their greeters obviously wondering who the female V.I.P. was, not recognizing her.

Or did they? A few people pointed and whispered.

What the hell *was* going on?

At the bottom of the escalator, Marion got her first clue. Outside the double set of double doors, a gaggle of reporters jockeyed for position, airport police and other suited agents keeping a path open to a plain government sedan, waiting under the Arrivals sign.

Marion slowed. "What...."

She was going to ask what was going on, but that hadn't gone so well before, so she went with, "What's all this for? Who's here?"

"You, ma'am," the marshal said as his agents stepped ahead to trigger the automatic doors, and they all moved as a swarm for the cool, dry autumn air of Virginia.

Phnongtuk's humidity would not be missed.

As Marion stepped outside, an agent by the plain sedan opened the back door while others concentrated on corralling the gaggle.

Marion's Marshal told her, "Don't stop. Don't talk to anyone. Don't answer any questions. Just get in the car, please."

Reporters shouted questions with such volume and intensity, overlapping to make discernment of any single "ask" impossible, so Marion did as instructed and moved straight for the open car door, unsettled. At this point, it looked inviting.

During her dash, Marion caught enough shouted words here and there to put together how they knew who she was.

"Mrs. Cooper over here!" Camera flashes popped like fireworks. "Marion! What was it like!" "What did you see?"

Something about "UFOs."

"Watch your head," the agent at the sedan said, as he gently placed his hand above Marion's nape and guided her into the cloth backseat of the black Impala.

Marion felt like a felon.

Once in the car, as the outside agent closed the door, relative peace returned.

———————

At another airport, O'Hare, halfway back across the country, Alanda was running her own gauntlet.

"Miss Borsomb, what was it like!" "Miss Borsomb, can you tell us what you saw!" "Mrs. Tucker, did your husband make it?" "Did they find him yet?" "Is he alive?"

"Can you describe the *spacemen*?"

On that, Alanda looked—and the flashes popped like roman candles, catching her looking like a startled, frightened doe as her six marshals led her to her black Impala sedan and her door agent told her to watch her head as he helped her inside to the quieter safety, the car pulling away before her door fully shut.

After getting a hundred more photos taken through the closed window, Alanda looked to find that she was three black-suited men long of being alone. The driver wore dark glasses, but she could tell he was checking her out in his rearview every few seconds.

Sitting next to him in the front seat sat a man who could have been a clone, only slightly larger—*fatter*, Alanda thought, as mean as she ever got—also wearing RayBan aviators but no seatbelt so that he turned easily in his seat towards her with a fixed smile.

Staring.

Alanda turned away from his unflinching gaze to the third, thinner man in the backseat with her—identical to the others, but Black. He, too, sat calmly observing her. He did not *feel* Black to Alanda as he wore the same stoic smile as the White men.

At least he was not wearing dark glasses.

———

In Marion's car on the east coast, her three men—two Black and one White—stared similarly. All of them had CIA written all over them. They may have claimed to be marshals, but Marion knew better. Having lived around D.C. all her life, she had seen many operatives in her forty-five years. Sure, they tried to lay low and blend in; but they all lived in McLean, Langley, or Bethesda—a dead giveaway.

That and the *attitude.*

The one in front on the passenger side, her seatbelt-less White guy, who had also spun around to stare, said, "You drew quite a crowd."

He said it as if he found humor in her situation—some agency hilarity, no doubt—comedy wasted on Marion. "Who are you, and why am I here?" she said.

"In this car?" he said.

Frustrated, tired, and more than a little overwhelmed, Marion said, "That, too."

"You don't mean 'back in America,'" he *guessed.*

"I would prefer it if we could dispense with the attempts at being clever and explain to me why—"

Now, Marion's handsome younger Black man without sunglasses in the backseat finished her question for her, "—you were met at the jetway, led out through the klatch of frothing reporters, thrown in a getaway car, and sped off to you-don't-know-where."

Marion stared, wide-eyed. He nailed it perfectly.

In *her* sedan, Alanda stared at her agent with the same confusion. He said, "Only for your safety, I assure you." He paused. "And to ask you a few questions."

"About?" Marion asked her man.

"Your trip."

"Of course," Marion said. Then, she slathered on her own sarcastic humor. "The earthquake that may not have been an earthquake at all—which I saw, felt, and experienced—and this crazy talk about 'alien invaders.' *That* trip?"

The front seat man offered a thin smile.

———————

Alanda had now noticed that their car was one of three. A large black SUV with blacked-out windows led, and another followed. She had never been in an official *convoy* before. "Where are you taking me?" she asked anyone in the car.

"Don't be frightened," the man in front said.

"Well, I am," she said.

"You needn't be," he assured her.

Alanda said emphatically, "I wish to be taken home, please. Right now."

"That's where we're taking you, ma'am," her driver said.

Alanda looked at her Black backseat companion. He nodded.

———————

Marion saw the news vans with pole antennas and swarms of reporters clustered on the sidewalks outside her house and down the street, all glued to their phones, with more arriving and rushing to set up.

"What the hell is going on?" Marion demanded of her handlers.

Men and women in black suits had hopped out of the leading and trailing SUVs, rushed back to open her door and formed a barricade to the front door.

Her backseat man said calmly. "We're going inside."

Marion said, "I would hope."

They did—amidst more shouted questions about natural disasters, armies, wars, and alien invaders.

Inside her front door, Marion had a one-word summation, "Jesus."

"Yep," her front seat man said. "Fuckin' vultures."

Marion snapped him a look, halfway expecting an apology, but all she got was a *That's the fuckin' way it is* smile.

Obviously, he did not regard the First Amendment in the same light as Marion Cooper. She said, "Why are there soldiers outside my front door?"

"Marines, ma'am. Back door, too," her backseat guy said. To which her front seat guy added, "Just for your protection, ma'am. Nothing nefarious."

"Protection against the free press vultures?" Marion said, snidely.

"Whoever, ma'am," he said in kind.

Marion did her best not to scowl and peered out her front drapes at the milling mass of reporters and military types in her front yard.

A new voice said, "Please, Mrs. Cooper, have a seat, please."

Marion turned to find three more agents already in her house, waiting. "Who are you?" she asked.

"Please, have a seat," the lead agent—a greying, solid White man in his mid-Fifties—said. The two other agents, both younger White women, indicated the couch, using their hands like Vanna White, pointing to a blank square.

Marion looked at them sternly, then sat on her couch—erect.

———————

Alanda's three-person interrogation team gave her the same treatment. When she did not sit, her lead—a clone of Marion's guy, only Black—said, "Please, this won't take long or be uncomfortable. I promise."

"Speak for yourself," Alanda said, feeling extreme discomfort. Why were these people already in her house? *How* were they in her house? And who the *hell* —

It hit her. "Oh my God," she said, paling. "He's dead."

She sat. Hard.

"Who's dead?" her guy asked.

"Lucas," she said.

"He's dead?" her man said. "How do you know that, Alanda?"

Alanda did not have an answer. "What?" she said, confused for a moment. Then she had another question, "How do you know so much about us? About me."

Marion knew why her interrogators knew so much about her. *It's what they do.* So, she didn't ask.

The man in the middle-shelf suit said, "I believe you know Sergeant Ashton Mosely."

"Know?" Marion said. "No." The man tilted his head. "Met?" Marion said. "Yes."

"I see," the agent acknowledged. And waited.

Marion understood. "He's the young soldier who helped us."

"Escape?" her man said.

"I suppose," Marion said. But wondered, "Was it an escape? From what were we escaping?"

"You were there," her man said. "You tell us."

"I think you know," Marion said — not sandbagging, but not wanting to play games.

"Fair enough," he said. "What was your...opinion of Sergeant Mosely."

Marion pondered several *perspectives*, then went with the harshest one. *Why not?* "I thought he was out of his mind," Marion said. Then, feeling bad having put it so severely, she added, "It's not surprising, given all that was going on."

"Going on?" the paunchy one said. He got a look from his superior and turned away, pretending to be interested in Marion's window treatments.

Marion glared at him, then told her lead agent, "Yes. Something to do with the hundred thousand dead bodies, *agent*."

He nodded banally, then suggested, "Let's focus on Sergeant Mosely."

Marion said, "He was scared, I think. Delusional. Seeing ghosts."

"And why would you think that, Marion?" her man asked, jotting a note in his little black book.

Marion paused. "I'd prefer you didn't call me by my first name."

"Okay," he said, looking up. "Mrs. Cooper."

Feeling she might be being led down some dark path—or something worse—Marion said, "Do I need a lawyer?"

"Why would you need a lawyer?" he asked.

Ruffling her feathers. "Look, agent...." She waited for a name. He did not give one. "Fine," she said. "Whatever your name is. I've been through hell. I saw things no human being should ever have to see, and my husband is probably dead."

"Why would you think that?" he asked.

Marion stared, wrestling with her inner demons and worst fears while fomenting a healthy loathing for the uninvited people in her living room.

———————

In Chicago, Alanda took a different tack. "He was nice," she said of Ashton Mosely. "He helped us."

"How?" her agent asked.

"He got us an earlier flight out, I think," she said. "He was very kind."

"What else?"

"What do you mean?"

"Did you notice anything unusual about him?"

"In what way?"

"In, let's call it, a hyperbolic way."

Alanda understood. "Oh," she said. "You mean the aliens and all that."

"All what?" he asked without moving.

Alanda asked her interrogator, "Why are you asking me all of this? I don't know any more than anyone else."

"But you were there. You saw things."

"Oh yeah," Alanda said—feeling that fear and sickness creeping over her, as it had with every memory or flash of an image that skipped through her mind.

"So, I'm just asking you how you would categorize Sergeant Mosely."

"Categorize?" Alanda said. "What do you mean? Is he in trouble for helping us out? He asked us not to say anything."

"Why is that?"

"I guess because he didn't want to get in *trouble*," Alanda said, growing equally frustrated with her questioner. He did not offer any explication as to Mosely's situation, so Alanda asked, "Is this going to take much longer?"

"It doesn't have to," Marion's man told her in answer to the same question.

Alanda's interrogator flipped to the next page of his notes and asked, "What can you tell me about your husband's interest in the CIA?"

Alanda was surprised—and cautious. "What do you mean?"

"He applied," the man said. "You did know that. Correct?"

"I suppose," Alanda said. "He never really talked about it. Just something in college." Sensing trouble of the conspiracy type, she said, "Is that what this is about? Did the CIA capture him or kill him or something? Is he a *secret agent*?"

On hearing the words come out of her own mouth, Alanda quickly realized that idea was dumb. "Of course, he isn't. That's ridiculous," she said, mostly for her own edification. But the notion quickly morphed into concern. "Wait. *Did* they kill him?"

"Who?"

"The CIA!"

"Why would the CIA do that, Alanda?"

———————

Marion faced down the same line of questioning about her man—but with less caution. "How long are we going to play this game, agent whoever? And please don't say 'as long as it takes.' I can assure you that my husband is not in the CIA and never has been. He's a business consultant for an international hardware manufacturer. He sells *copper* to developing economies. Hardly the stuff of a spy novel. He's so boring we've had to buy books to spice up our sex life." She looked her man straight in the eye. "Happy now?" she said.

Obviously, she was *not*.

"Oh," Marion added. "And he started out in exotic lumber purchasing—until the international community made it too difficult to export. If that helps. Wood. Before the metal." And again, she *clarified*, "Copper."

Marion had clearly moved from trying to be helpful—to

not.

Her man smiled—patronizingly, she thought—then asked, "What about Dan's activities outside work?"

Before Marion could object to his casual name reference, he said, "Mr. Cooper. I'm sorry." He pressed on. "Anything unusual? Friends, say. Late nights unaccounted for? That kind of thing."

Marion flushed. Angry. "I believe we've talked enough about my husband. If you find him, please send him home to me in one piece—after you interrogate him, of course. Do you guys still do anal probes, or is that only the *'aliens.'*"

The agent remained unruffled. "We're just trying to get a fuller picture of why you might have been in Phnongtuk at this particular time."

"We were on vacation," Marion said. "It was there or Alaska in winter or another goddamned bar in Cozumel packed with drunken Fall Breakers. Or Detroit. He did offer Detroit. But I'm not a big Packard fan. So, which would you choose, Agent Nobody with No Name?"

"I understand," the mystery *marshal* said and made a note. "That was a big factory, up there, that Packard building. Biggest ever, as I recall."

"I couldn't care less," Marion said, feeling that if her face became any more pinched, she would look like a dehydrated orange.

Then, despite her doubt that it was possible, Marion bristled even more and said, "I believe I have the right to have an attorney present."

And she shut up.

Her man said—with the same patronizing smile—said, "This doesn't involve the law, Marion."

Amazingly — to Marion — she bristled even *more*. "Apparently *not*," she said.

And really clammed up.

Her agent chuckled as if he had to admit that she got him on that one. "Well," he said. "We're really more interested in Sergeant Mosely."

"So, you're not marshals. Are you Army intel?" Marion said, flatly. "CIA?"

"I'm just someone asking questions," he said.

But Marion Cooper knew he was much more than that — and much more dangerous.

In Chicago, Alanda said, "Like I said, Ashton was very nice. He helped us when no one else would."

"Why do you think that is?" her man asked.

"I don't know," Alanda said. "He's a decent human being?" She, too, had turned sour. The agents were losing their interrogatees.

Time to close.

"What did you think when he proffered the possibility of aliens? Did you believe him?"

Alanda said, "I don't know what I thought. Anything's possible, I suppose. We can't be the only sentient creatures in the universe."

"So, you believed him."

"I didn't say that."

Her agent nodded, then asked, "Have you seen the news?"

Alanda said, "The TVs didn't work on our plane, and you kidnapped me from the airport before I could see a TV there."

"It wasn't kidnapping, Alanda. It was for your own good. You saw those reporters. They would have eaten you alive."

Alanda felt feisty. "I doubt that, but okay, I'll bite. What are they wanting to report that has anything to do with me or Ashton or *visitors from outer space*?"

After a moment of meeting her gaze, the agent nodded to a waiting female agent who turned on her television set and ran through channels, every one of which had only one topic to report...

———————

A network anchor spoke into the camera, saying, "Release of the controversial images has brought mixed reactions."

A congresswoman on the capitol building steps, telling a reporter, "I haven't seen the actual footage, so I have no statement at this time."

A Senator hurrying through the rotunda, past John Adams, said, "No comment at this time. Thank you."

A spokeswoman for the Whitehouse said, "We have no official response at this time."

A Representative from Missouri getting on the capitol elevator waved "no" and said, "Nothing at this time," as the door closed to hide him.

Reactions on the street ran in a different direction.

A generic New Yorker glared and walked away without comment.

A Brooklynite said, "Aliens?!" The remainder of his comment, though he looked amused, was a series of bleeps. He walked away, waving his hand and laughing.

A Florida woman in an old red hat said, "Doesn't surprise me. Way the things are these days. It's disgraceful." Hard to tell if she understood the question in the first place.

A "Mountain Man" in Idaho said, "Those people over there? Sounds like a good solution. Take 'em *all* out." His wife laughed with him. Their T-shirts said it all—if one could read through the blurred-out parts.

A woman in Southern California wearing something multi-layered, multi-hued, and otherwise confusing said, "Oh, I'm sure of it. We've been waiting. They have come. Our prayers have been answered."

On CNN, Wolf Blitzer presented a typically stoic, "The State Department has denounced the images as 'fraudulent, disturbing, and irrelevant.' Yet hostilities continue to mount between the North and South. We return to our panel after the break."

CBS had a "reporter on the ground" in Phnongtuk, getting responses from locals—a translator heard in a voiceover saying, "I believe the photos are real and that the North is working with the creatures from other galaxies to destroy our country with natural disasters. My family is leaving to Myanmar, where it is safer."

ABC had a reporter at Miami International Airport, holding up a mic' to a young hat-backwards tourist who said, "Yeah, a friend of mine shot some stuff with her cellphone, just before the quake, and you can see...*something*. I mean, I didn't think it was a UFO, but I don't know. It's pretty sketchy. And they confiscated her phone."

Reporter: "Who confiscated her phone?"

Tourist: "The government, man. Who else?"

Reporter: "Ours or theirs?"

Tourist: "How would I know? Soldiers came into the room at the airport where they had us and took her phone. Then they put her on a different plane. I think they did. Anyway, I didn't see her anymore. I don't know where she is—what they did to her."

He broke into tears.

Back in the newsroom, the ABC anchor said into camera, "That was David Matheson, from Teaneck, New Jersey, earlier today. Reports are that *he* has now been reported missing by his family."

Marion Cooper watched in silence, unmoved, then said, "What does and of this have to do with me? I didn't see any aliens. I can tell you that. Just an earthquake and a tsu—"

"That's fine," her agent told her. "We're more concerned with your impressions of Sergeant Mosely."

"I've already covered that," Marion said flatly. "I have nothing else to say. No other opinions. He helped us try to find our husbands, then get a flight out. Other than that, he sounded like any other Alex Jones conspiracy nut. Are you booting him out of the Army? Giving him a Section 8? I'd prefer not to testify and ruin some young man's life if you don't mind."

"That would not be my job, ma'am," her agent said. "Above my pay-grade."

The two female agents grinned.

Marion's mien made it clear she was done humoring them or answering any-damn-thing else.

Alanda offered one more comment about young Ashton. "He said that it could have been some kind of secret weapon—a beam or something that can cause a natural disturbance. Like a laser, I suppose. He was scared, I can tell you that."

"Scared of the weapon or afraid that he had told you something he shouldn't?"

"Both," Alanda said.

Two of the agents shared a look.

She saw it. "Look, I don't really remember," she said, trying to cover--poorly. "*I* was scared. He was scared. We all were. It was...scary. He could have said anything, and I would have believed him. At least considered it. Look, I just...I just want...."

Alanda was crying instantly. She said, "I just want my Lucas back."

———————

Marion's agent seemed to understand that he wasn't going to get any more from her and stood. "We're going to ask you not to go out for a while. We'll have guards posted 24/7."

"Why?"

"Just a precaution."

"Against what?"

"Whatever. This is a live situation. Unfolding. So, until we know you're safe—"

"Which will be when? You said I *am* safe."

"We'll let you know, Marion. Mrs. Cooper. Until then, your cellphones and your landlines have been nulled."

"Nulled," Marion repeated sourly. "How am I supposed to get ahold of my sister?"

"She'll be notified."

"Of what?"

"Your situation—your...brief quarantine, if you will."

"And?"

"She will be free to come and go—after a few weeks, I would guess."

"After a few...." Marion shook her head. She knew there was no point in arguing or even discussing her situation with these *sycophantic droogs*. "Fine, just go," she said and stood.

"May I use my own bathroom, or will I need an escort in there as well. In case it isn't safe. Did you check the shower for Anthony Perkins?"

Her agent offered the same insincere smile and said, "Your refrigerator is full. Same with the freezer and the cabinets. We checked your grocery receipts and bought more of the same — plus some extra ice cream."

He smiled. She didn't.

He said, "If you need anything else, just ask whoever's outside your door, and we'll see that you get it as quickly as possible. Until then, just hold tight, and we'll have this figured out as soon as we can and get your life back to normal."

"With Dan?" Marion said.

Her agent's face revealed no promise, no emotion. He said, "We hope so, Mrs. Cooper. But...."

"I shouldn't count on it."

The agents said nothing more and filed out. Marion Cooper watched *the bastards* go — and contrived an escape plan.

13

The night was hot and still, oppressively humid. Dan's arms hurt. His body hurt. His face hurt. His brain felt numb, emotions on hold for twelve days. He kept count. The longest twelve days in his life, without qualification.

A loud clang awoke him from a sleep he had not recognized. There followed loud shouting amidst the shuffling of many feet.

Lucas's cries came next. "No! Stop! What are you doing?! Dan! DAN!"

Though Dan gave loud encouragements for Lucas to "Hang in there, Lucas," he was not sure Lucas could hear. "Try not to fight them," he said, louder.

"Dan! Help me! Stop them!"

There followed thumps and cracks and screams. Then the sound of feet scraping—Lucas being dragged from his cell, screaming, begging for help, for mercy.

Receiving none.

The guards that Dan could not see but knew were in and out of the next cell over said nothing—did their job, spiriting young Lucas away in the night. Silence fell again.

No one came for Dan.

Three days passed before a powerful tropical storm hit the compound. Rain poured through the gaps in the rebar overhead without obstruction. Dan stood in puddles that covered the floor, wall to wall, hoping none of the wild lightning crackling overhead would hit those metal bars and travel down to his feet.

He was spared electrocution when, as had happened with Lucas, his cell door clanged open, and several masked and silent guards poured in. Too many to offer any resistance.

After releasing him from his chained bonds, the unspeaking men dragged Dan, limp and naked, out of the cell and away. At some point, he passed out.

Dan awoke in a covered hallway, mostly dry. He could still hear the torrential rain, lashing winds, and throbbing thunder as if it was inside the hall rather than out.

"Ah," his original interrogator said, still masked. "Good," he said and nodded to the phalanx of hidden-faced soldiers who responded by jerking Dan up by his elbows and dragging him several yards down the dry floor to where two other guards waited at an open cell door, ready to assist or slam it shut on command. Maybe on Dan's hand or his head. He had no hope of any shows of kindness at this point.

They did not disappoint, catching him squarely across his spine as his keepers stood him up for entry into whatever they had in store for him, next.

Through glazed, barely focused eyes—nearly blind with pain—Dan looked up to see Lana, also nude and bruised, hanging from the wall by her wrists. Half her hair had been shorn. The remaining half hung clumped, stringy, filthy.

On hearing the clamor, Lana looked up, her eyes no clearer than Dan's. She smiled and said, "I wondered where you were."

"Silence!" Dan's interrogator told her.

"Fuck you," she said—and received a cane swipe for her impudence. She refused to let them know her pain. Dan could see the determination in her clenched jaw.

The Interrogator then nodded his men toward the side wall, where they dragged Dan and secured him by his wrists. Better than elbows. He allowed them their way.

"Nice abs," Lana said. "You work out?"

Before he knew it, Dan had chuckled—and they both received warning slaps.

Though they had been told not to speak, when their cruel new masters left the covered cell—at least it had a roof—Dan said, "Nice place. Come here often?"

"First time," she said.

Dan said, "I like what you did with the place."

"Not bad, considering my budget," she said.

"I like the ceiling. My accommodations were lacking."

"Wet," she said.

"Very," he said.

"Yeah," she said. "I was in one of those until an hour ago." Then she said, "I think it was an hour. Might have been a month."

Dan stood more erect than he had been left, his strength greater than his previous display. He chuckled again. He knew the feeling of time loss well.

"What do you think we're in for?" he asked her.

"Damned if I know," Lana said. "Wrong place, wrong time."

Dan nodded and asked her how she was doing.

"Holding up," she said, referencing her restraints, getting another chuckle from Dan, who had to admire her grace under pressure. "You?" she asked him.

"Time'a my life," Dan said. "What do you figure they have on us?"

"Nothing," his cellmate said without hesitation.

"So, why do you think they brought us here?" Dan said.

"They were bored?" Lana said. "Needed some excitement?"

Dan said, "As if all that back there wasn't exciting enough."

"Praise the lord and pass the biscuits," Lana said, shaking her head. "Shit was rough."

Dan had another question. "What do you figure they have in mind for us?"

"No idea," Lana said. "But it's probably not going to be the most fun I ever had in chains."

A few moments passed as each assessed their thoughts and futures. Then Lana said, "They're *listening*." She nodded up.

Dan looked up to see that this cell also had rebar hatchwork that hung down, but here, under a solid cement roof. A foot of air separated the two, in which were four cameras placed at each corner of the room, pointing in so as not to miss anything.

Dan said, "Don't know what they expect to hear."

"Anything that gives them an excuse to terrorize us some more."

Dan nodded wearily. He knew that he could take more, though if he was honest with himself, he didn't know how much. He always figured he had a strong constitution, but this was something else. Beyond the pale.

"You holding up okay?" Lana asked him.

"About like you, I guess."

"At least you got to see me naked," she said.

"Hmm," was all he had for her. Then he added, "Hadn't really noticed."

"Wow," she said. "You really know how to impress a lady."

"If that lady was my wife," he said.

Lana smiled. "Nice turnaround."

"Thank you," Dan said, and that ended their patter.

Elsewhere, a guard in headphones dozed off.

Cold water awakened Dan and Lana the next morning. Both squirmed to avoid taking any down their throats into their lungs while trying to protest. But their "All rights!" and "Enoughs!" went unyielded.

After half a minute, the water stopped, the door was unlocked, and a new masked Interrogator—a shorter one in a military uniform—entered with an entourage of guards who looked ready to do any awful bidding he might request.

He said, in less-perfect English than the black-bandana'd interrogator, "So. You have gotten to know each other better, I hear."

"You didn't hear shit," Lana said.

"Oh, we heard it all."

"Then you heard that we knew you were hearing it."

"That, too," the masked military man said, unbothered. "Everything will come to an end."

Dan said, "What is that supposed to mean?"

"We shall see," their captor replied—and moved closer, his posse alert. "I think I have made my point," he said.

Dan said, "And that is?"

"You are here—and you will not be leaving."

"Is that a death threat?" Dan said.

"We will have to see," the masked man said.

Dan nodded at their inquisitor's uniform and said, "Okay, general."

That seemed to stop the shortish man. He looked down at his epaulets, as if he could see the stars on his collar and said, "And how is it that you would recognize the military decorations of my country?"

"I don't," Dan said. "I meant it as an insult. But thanks for the confirmation."

"Ouch," Lana said. "Gotcha." Then she added, "Hey. Ever hear of the Peter Principle?" Then she said, "Nah. That's probably *over your head.*"

This time, Dan laughed. "Good one," he said.

"Thank you, thank you," Lana said.

The general smiled — at least it appeared so under his thin mask. "Yes, you two…."

They knew it was coming. One nod, and both received solid blows. Then, the command came to stand down in local parlance. His men stepped back.

The general sucked his teeth like a southern redneck sheriff in a bad chase movie, cocking his head as he was apparently wont to do, as if deciding whether his prisoners had had enough or needed more to be submissive enough for this day.

After several moments of contemplation, he nodded — this time to himself — and gave an order that resulted in both Dan and Lana being released from their bonds and ordered to sit on the concrete floor.

The general said, "I will say this only once. You will do as I ask; you will answer all of my questions, or you will die in this room."

Satisfied with his welcome speech, he turned and walked

out. His guards followed. As their steps faded—and did not return—Dan allowed himself to stretch his aching limbs and stand—unimpeded by restraints. He stood. It felt like being reborn.

He groaned with satisfaction, and Lana joined him, seeming to equally enjoy her freedom—as it were. "I think a hug is in order," she said and held out her hands.

"Maybe later," Dan said, indirectly referring to their nakedness.

"They want you to fuck me," she said. "Get us to dime."

"Why would… 'fucking' do that?"

"Ask the primitive mind," Lana said, sardonically. "Typical macho bullshit. See, if women ran torture programs, we'd threaten to withhold coffee and chocolate."

"We get coffee here?" Dan said.

After a few steps that apparently felt *better* than being reborn, Lana said, "They think that if we have sex, I will become attached to you, and that will make me talk. To save you. Or, that if you become attached to me, *you* will talk when they torture me in front of you."

Dan grunted and said, "I guess we can expect that."

"But only if you fuck me," Lana said with a wry smile.

She had spunk, and Dan had an appreciation for that. But he said, "Don't hold your breath."

"Happily married?" she said.

"Very," he said.

Lana walked and stretched some more. "Didn't really look that way, I have to say."

"That would be none of your business, would it?" he said.

"Not really," Lana seemed to agree. "Unless we want to live—and maybe even get out of here."

"I wouldn't count on either," he said.

"The fucking, the living, or the being released," she said.

"Right," he said.

She said, "You're funny. I didn't expect that."

Dan said with no humor, "Laughter makes the world go 'round."

Lana chuckled, said, "It's the best medicine," sardonically. "I saw that in *Reader's Digest*."

She did some deep squats to stretch out her hamstrings. "So, you're not going to fuck me even if it means saving your life."

"Not yet," Dan said, and she laughed again — continuing her squats. He said, "Could you turn the other way when you do that?"

Lana looked down at her bare vulva. "You don't like my laser work? It cost a small fortune. But it's worth it not to have to shave. I'm surprised you don't like it. Most guys do."

"I didn't say that," he said.

"So, you *are* considering fucking me," she said with a hint of glee at *catching* him.

"I think we've discussed that angle enough," he said.

"Fine with me," she said. "I just want to live and see the light of day again."

"Me too," he assured her.

"So," she said, standing. "You have an alternate plan?"

Dan looked up at the cameras and said, "Not yet."

Lana nodded, strolling to stretch out the rest of her aching muscles. "You're indecisive on many issues."

"Not really," Dan said. "Just patient."

"Cogitating."

"Something like that."

She stopped in front of him, staring. So, he asked her, "Do *you* have a plan?"

Lana said. "Not yet," and walked on. Talking on the move, "Though I have to say, I think we should fuck and get it over with. Prove them wrong."

Dan watched her, not watching him. "As I mentioned...."

"You're married. Marion, was it?"

"Yes. Happily married, despite what you thought you saw. You?"

"Divorced. *Very* happily so."

"Not a nice guy?" Dan said.

Lana ran her fingers across the cement walls as she walked the perimeter of their cell. "Let's just say, he made these jerks look like saints."

"Abuser?" Dan said.

"Sadistic, nasty bastard."

"Sounds like them."

"Believe me. 'Law enforcement.'"

"Mmm."

Seeing her stroll had an appeal to Dan, so he joined her, a few steps behind, feeling his lower legs for the first time in days.

It felt marvelous—so good that Dan did not notice Lana stop, and he ran into her, his body making head-to-heel contact with her bare skin. "Sorry," he said, reflexively.

Lana turned around and grabbed onto him, preventing him from pulling away. She said, "Does this mean you've already changed your mind?"

Dan's features hardened—but nothing else. "No," he said. But he did not move. Lana Yarborough was an attractive woman—even bruised, beaten, and humiliated.

"Think about it," she said, holding her naked flesh against

his.

"Probably won't," he said. When she feigned disappointment, he said, "Sorry. Not the most romantic place I've ever been."

"Who said anything about romance?" she said. "You ever been to a singles bar late on a Saturday night?"

"Right," he said. "But still, no."

Lana said, more seriously, "You do realize we are never getting out of here alive, right? I mean, you do understand that, yes?"

Dan Cooper stared into the shadowy blue depths of Lana's eyes, as deep into her soul as he could, and said, "No."

The moment held. Then she said, "Well, you better," and walked away.

Marion Cooper put on her pajamas and prepared to climb into bed alone for the twenty-third time since getting back to the States. She had not yet been allowed to leave her house. Marines still guarded her doors, her landline was still dead, and all electronic devices had been removed. She had no contact with her sister, with Alanda, or anyone else in the outside world.

Bored out of her mind, Marion had cleaned the house top-to-bottom six times. Still, she felt she was holding up well, considering.

Then she ran across a photo of herself and Dan in Trinidad, on vacation, on their way to Colombia, in the south, near Venezuela, and across to a godforsaken little nothing of a town called La Vaca.

"The cow," they had laughed every time they heard someone say the name of the place—a classic Banana Republic kind of village with a dusty square, a nice hotel, and a cheap one filled with ex-pats on the run from something—street vendors selling everything from flowers to sandals to coca leaves. They stayed the week in the nice hotel, and Marion enjoyed their time there, even if Dan went off twice on hardware business.

The jungle wrapped all around, the air clear, the sun hot, and the humidity bearable. Marion remembered her smile in the photo as the last one she felt good about—deep and satisfied. Then things got complicated, and she and Dan seemed to be drifting apart.

This last trip halfway around the world held her last glimmer of hope for bringing them back together. But the magic had not returned. The emptiness lingered, and Marion had all but given up hope things would ever be good again—that love would ever be reborn.

Then, the horrors.

Sitting on the edge of her tall Stearns-Foster, feet barely able to reach the floor, that happy photo in her hand—both of them smiling—Marion was transported back in time and feelings. Back into their past, even before the photo that represented all that had come before and would come after that, she could not have anticipated in that moment.

And she wept.

14

In a town south of the Phnongtuk — one not hit as hard — many of the buildings still stood, if slightly damaged. Most of the powerlines remained, one of them going to an appliance store, in the window of which a television aired some breaking news.

A crowd gathered to watch a northern military leader shouting into the camera, tapping on a map with a pointer, apparently threatening the inhabitants of a town.

This town.

The screen then cut to what appeared to be dodgy images, likely from a shaky cellphone aimed upward as slender silver objects flitted past overhead.

The oddly shaped *aircraft* flew by so quickly as to lack certitude of their origin, intent, or design. But the strange screeching sounds they made onscreen made them formidable and frightening to the group watching the TV as the northern officer returned to scream more threats, this time beating the map of their area with his pointer.

A moment later, the ground began to shake violently, and the television set fell off its pedestal, crashing onto the floor behind the window, which also shattered, sending large shards bursting out.

Villagers scrambled away a fast-approaching roar became one of the screeching silver flying things, so low as to be undefinable, almost *unseeable* — their sound a mix of a jet-like roar and the shrieking of a giant movie Godzilla creature. A second after that, an explosion sent everyone not already running scattering for cover, for home, for safety. Anywhere but where they had been.

Seconds after that, the store exploded and turned to rubble.

As citizens ran pell-mell through the streets, army transports and armed vehicles appeared, seemingly from nowhere, to fire up at the now-empty sky. The only sound louder than their heavy-caliber weapons came from the sky as, seconds later, the strange silver flying objects screeched back overhead in the opposite direction, so low they seemed to touch the swaying palms.

More explosions followed.

Two tanks went up in balls of exploding shrapnel. Three transport trucks filled with soldiers and civilians simply evaporated — lost to flame and fury.

And the ground shook. And shook. And shook....

———————

In the bar of a mostly undamaged hotel several kilometers away, a local bartender and two Europeans in blue United Nations shirts watched footage of the earlier attack in the other town — handheld video of shaking buildings, explosions, burning military vehicles, and blurry flash-images of low-flying silver objects racing across the scene before they could be identified or seen clearly, their sounds unworldly and piercing.

The report cut to the same screaming northern officer

from before, waving his pointer, beating his pointer, slapping his pointer across a map of the just-attacked town, while subordinates stood to the side, stern and unwavering in their threatening intensity.

No smiling allowed.

The two UN men shared an anxious look. The bartender saw their concern—then his own dread escalated as they all heard a rumbling outside, followed by pounding boots, and the door flew open. The bartender backed up, afraid, and the UN men swore, without looking back.

"*Scheize*," one said.

The soldiers grabbed the two men off their barstools, despite their dual protests in German, French, and regional pigeon, and dragged the two peacekeepers out. The bartender heard their continued protestations—silenced by a single gunshot.

The trucks rumbled away as quickly as they had arrived.

———————

Marion Cooper's flat screen TV flickered to life—her cable back on—catching a network anchor mid-report.

"...State Department has closed the embassy and removed personnel. All foreign nationals, including peacekeeping troops and aid workers, have been ordered out of the country. War has swept the small nation like wildfire. Thousands more are believed dead. Many there are blaming the casualties on paranormal activities and as-yet unidentified 'super-weapons.' Luci Singh has this report from Washington."

Marion sat on her couch to watch. She had not seen any news in weeks.

Luci Singh, an Asian reporter of indeterminate specific lineage, held a microphone up for the same Congresswoman who now had something to say. "No one is being let in or out.

The entire country has been closed down and sealed off. They are at war, and neither side wants any contact with outside nation states."

Singh asked, "When do you expect there to be a break in the action?"

"We have no idea," the Congresswoman said. "We've had no diplomatic interaction or conversations. No one in the country, no cellphone coverage. All the towers have been disabled. We don't even know for sure who got out and who's still there."

"Is there a plan to get our people out?"

"I can't comment on that, but I will say that we expect this situation to continue."

"For how long?"

"Again, we don't know. It could end tomorrow or go on for months. Years, maybe. If you remember, the war in Syria had been raging for five years before we even *discussed* getting involved. And even then, our response was limited, long in coming, and ultimately fruitless."

Singh pointed out, "In that case, we had U.N. inspectors giving us some clues."

The congresswoman said, "But even then, we could not rely on those reports."

"And you're getting no reports at all in this case."

"None whatsoever. A complete blackout."

After getting a prompt in her earpiece, Singh framed her next question carefully. "There have been reports of aliens and UFOs—strange New Age weapons no one has ever seen before or even heard about. What can you tell us about these rumors?"

The Congresswoman stiffened, anxious. "I have no comment on that. Again, we have no one on the ground and satellite intelligence is of little use in such a densely forested part of the world. We just hope it remains contained."

"The attacks? The war? The weapons?"

The congresswoman started away. "That's all I have to say for now. Thank you." She trotted up the steps to hide from reporters.

Luci Singh turned to the camera. "There you have it, Donald—as much as it is. Luci Singh outside Congress—"

Marion switched off the broadcast, unsure if she was happy to have it back or not. But mainly, Had she been wrong about Ashton Mosely's warnings?

Figuring there was only one person she could trust in this regard, Marion hurried into her bedroom, where she dug out a scrap of paper she had secreted away from her questioning agents, Alanda's phone number. Maybe she had heard something more.

Marion reached for her phone, familiarly on the nightstand, forgetting it was still gone. She could *get* news, just not share it.

15

Blinding light and blaring regional rock music filled their cell. Kliegs and speakers had been erected outside the cage to pour in the audio-visual pain.

At least they had been given clothes.

Lana shouted, "They could at least play some Zeppelin."

Dan replied, "You like Zeppelin?"

"No," she shouted. "Hate 'em. But it would be better than this whiny shit."

Dan still had enough hope to chuckle. They had been rehung on adjoining walls, so they had little else to laugh about.

Suddenly, the music stopped, and the lights clacked off. Impenetrable darkness and quiet enveloped them.

After several moments of silent gratitude, Lana said, "How ya hangin'?"

"Same," Dan said with another appreciative chuckle. "You?"

"Stroll in the park, day at the beach, piece'a cake. Take your pick," she said, her voice thin in the black stillness.

When they heard footsteps, Dan said, "Here we go again."

A moment later, the lights came back on, illuminating their cell like Dodger Stadium during the Series.

Lana said, "They don't know anything, and we don't have anything to tell them."

Dan said, "I think they see it differently."

"Well," she said, "fuck 'em."

Masked soldiers stepped in front of the kliegs and threw the locks. After the masked general stepped in, his men followed and stayed close, as always.

He walked directly to Lana and said, "We are through playing games."

"Aw, don't stop now," she said. "It was just getting interesting."

The general nodded at one of his soldiers, who then punched her.

"Hey!" Dan objected.

Two soldiers punched him.

The general said, "Time has run out for you."

Dan groaned and said, "You use a lot of clichés. Anyone ever tell you that?"

The general nodded for his goons to step in, but Lana yelled, "Cut it out! He doesn't know anything!"

"Lies!" the general shouted. "You are both spies!"

"*What*?" Dan said, sounding incredulous. "Is that what this bullshit is? You think we're *spies*?" He laughed. "We're not fucking *spies*. What the fuck are you thinking?"

The general strode over to him. "We do not use such foul language in our country. It is forbidden by law. Anyone using such language is subject to punishment."

"What do you call what you've already been doing?" Dan said.

The general warned, "Oh, this is nothing. What is ahead for you if you don't tell us what we want to hear will make this seem like a happy massage."

Lana said, sounding frustrated, "Just...tell me what you want to hear, and I'll say it. Okay? How's that?"

"Better," the general said.

He turned back to Dan. "But it is not what we *want* to hear. It is what we know we are *going* to hear."

Dan shook his head and said, "See? Clichés."

The general continued, unbothered. "We will use all the clichés available to us, I assure you. We have seen your filthy American movies and made many notes."

Lana said, "Is this where you bring out the battery cables?"

The general had only one phrase, "C-I-A."

Dan said, "You're CIA?"

The general gave a scornful chuckle. "That is who *you* are."

Dan laughed! He said, "Are you kidding me? Is that what you think?" He looked down and shook his head. "I'm in hardware consulting—pretty damn dull stuff—on *vacation*, and she's in fucking *cardboard* sales, for fuck's sake. Cardboard!" He laughed again.

The general continued to be unbothered. "I warned you about your language, American pig."

Dan said, "American pig? Really? CIA? Jesus. One cliché after another."

"Yes," the general said. "And we are just getting started." He strolled over to Lana. "You are CIA. We have no question in this matter."

Lana said, "You should because it's ridiculous. I don't even *know* anyone who's...in that. How would I? I don't even know what it is except *what I* see in the movies. And it doesn't look like this, I can tell you that." She shook her head. "I'm not in the CIA or FBI or anything else. I don't even like *cops*. Talk about 'pigs.'" She grunted a laugh. "If you ask me, you're the pig, here. Not Mr. Cooper, 'hardware salesman at large.'"

Another laugh from her drew the general's rage. "You lie!" he shouted — and nodded to her guard, who reached over and tore her shirt open and then off.

"Not this again," she said.

Dan's ire flared. "You can't do this. We're American citizens!"

"You are CIA!"

Dan shouted back, "No! I'm *not*. I sell non-precious metals for hardware applications. That's all. No CIA or contact with them or anything else."

"Maybe you are not," the general said. "But she is."

Dan said, shaking his head, "She sells cardboard. She's not a goddamn spy."

"And I am not a flying nun," the general said.

Dan looked up. "That doesn't even make sense."

"It will," the general said. "And you see, I know much about American culture."

Dan said, "That was back in the 1960s, dude."

The general said, "And nothing has changed. You Americans still think nuns can fly and spies can go anywhere they like in the world and do whatever they like — cause ruin and chaos."

Dan said, "Is that with a K? As in *Get Smart*. That was big in the Sixties, too."

Lana said to Dan, "How do you even know that? How old *are* you?"

"Old enough," Dan said. "Reruns."

He turned back to the general. "Do you have any idea what our government will do to you when they find out what you did to *us*? To American citizens. On vacation. Working to provide your country with tourist revenue and…cardboard boxes?"

The general said with full arrogance, "They will do nothing."

Dan said, "I wouldn't count on that."

"I count on it with all my fingers and toes," the general said.

Dan rolled his eyes.

The general said, "Spies do not receive preferential treatment in any country." Then he laughed. "Ah, but I have *misspoken*."

Lana said, "There's a surprise."

The general told her, "Spies…receive the *worst* treatment. Until they *confess*."

Dan said, "There's nothing to confess!"

"You continue to LIE!" the general screamed again, losing control. And he yelled orders to his soldiers, who stripped off Lana's shorts and Dan's.

Naked again. "Great, perfect," he said.

The general said, suddenly calm again, "Are you not more comfortable without the burden of that heavy clothing? Surely, you must be cooler without them. Are not Americans foul nudists by nature? Taking photographs of their bare flesh in our most sacred of temples. Disrespecting our traditions. Our ways."

"That would not be me," Dan said. "I'm just your average, boring, sit at the bar and be happy I'm away on vacation kind of tourist. I don't even do the temple tours."

Lana told the general, "Maybe you should try visiting those temples, yourself. Praying a little might make you more humane. Follow those traditions."

"I do not need to pray," the general said. "I follow orders. And my orders are to get you to answer our questions. To tell us why you are here and what you know. When you do that, you will be set free to return to your filthy American ways." He paused. "Unless, of course, you admit that you are spies. Then you will be shot. Mercifully."

Dan said, "That's a real incentive, there."

The general showed his false smile. "It will be much more 'humane' than what we are going to do to you if you don't tell us all that we wish to know."

"There's nothing to tell!" Dan said. "Nothing to 'know'!"

"What he said," Lana said with wry detachment.

The general took a stroll around the cell, putting on his interrogator mien. "There is one thing we know. One thing we all know. And that is what American women want. What they all want."

Dan looked up, sharply. "Oh. You can't be serious."

"Oh, but I can," the general said. "And I am."

Dan said, "Geneva conventions? International agreements?"

"Do not apply," the general said. "Not to spies."

"We're not spies, goddammit!"

The general stopped pacing and grunted. He waved toward the bars. A guard opened the cell door, and two other masked men brought in a low table fitted with leather restraints.

"Really?" Dan said, barely holding back his loathing. "Which movie did you get that from? James Bond? No one tortures spies anymore. They deport them." He nodded at the table. "That crap doesn't even work. Read the reports. Try candy."

The general grunted and walked around the table, ending

up in front of Lana.

She said, "You don't scare me with that." She had her verve back, her defiance. "I dated an *insurance salesman* who had one of those in his basement."

The general said, "Then I'm sure you're familiar with how this particular piece of furniture works."

"Oh yeah. He liked me to strap him down on it and use a dildo on him."

The general nodded dispassionately and said, "We will leave it here so that you can contemplate *other* uses for it—with the tables turned."

Lana said, "Another cliché. By the way, turned out he was impotent. Can we look forward to that, too?"

The general offered a thin smile and then turned to Dan. "And so you won't feel left out of the festivities."

On his cue, another guard brought in a car battery with cables attached.

Now, Lana protested. "That's not even funny."

"It is not meant to be," the general said as his men set the battery down in front of Dan and then walked away.

Lana said, nastily, "Hey, asshole. *Americans.* Are you even hearing that? Does it mean anything at all to your tiny little prehistoric brain?"

The general said, "Ah, yes. The Americans with their strong sense of fair play, and your Geneva Conventions…in Abu Ghraib."

He moved to stand over the battery and said of the setup, "Was this not your American method of protecting humanity there? After the waterboarding, the parading around proud Muslim men in the nude—a shame they could never live down on this earth? *Those* American principles?"

He scoffed. "Your people thought this was a good way to get to the truth. Your Dick Cheneys and your Donald Rumsfelds. Your John Boltons. Your George *Bush*. Your racist soldiers. We are just following their methods to get at the truth. Only we will not be so stupid as to take *selfies* for posterity. We will leave that to the American hoodlums and terrorists."

The masked general turned away. "You see, we learned from the best. You were good teachers, you American barbarians. The best! We have only improved on it. Perfected it, if you will. We know what works, and we will do whatever is needed to find the truths we seek."

Dan shook his head, sourly. "You're a sick pup, general."

The general said, "I expected no less from you when confronted with your own sick American methods."

"I didn't have anything to do with that," Dan said. "None of us did. Not her, not three-hundred-thirty million other American citizens. That was a few rogue soldiers who were punished for their illegal actions. None of us regular Americans supported what they did."

The general said, "There is nothing 'regular' about you, sir. And certainly nothing 'regular' about Ms. Yarborough, here—or our representative who will become her new friend should she continue to be *uncooperative*." He turned toward the hallway.

Guards outside the cell waved to one side, and a large man dressed only in a sheer robe stepped into the open doorway—tall, muscular, and fit. Backlight from the kliegs revealed an extremely long and thick shadow between his legs.

Dan said, "Oh, come on. Seriously? What kind of military *leader* would approve anything like that?"

"One who has run out of options and needs to know what he needs to know."

Dan said, "In America? That you slander? You would be sent to Leavenworth and stripped of your command—forever. Maybe hanged."

"Thankfully, I do not have your lying, hypocritical 'leaders' to answer to," the general said. "Who only admit the truth of what they do in their CIA 'black sites' when *caught*." The general looked at Lana with a self-satisfied smirk.

She nodded over at the silent potential rapist and said of his appendage, "That thing doesn't scare me. Where'd he get it? Micronesia?" Dan chuckled at her courage and defiance. She added, "I've seen chihuahuas hung better."

The general appeared nonplussed. He said only, "We shall see."

Dan struggled against his chains. "Goddammit. This is fucked up. You've gone too far. You can't do this. It's wrong. She's a woman, for fuck's sake!"

"Humorous that you would choose to use that term," the general said.

Dan stood firm. "You *cannot* do this. It's inhuman. Disgusting. *Illegal!*"

The general said only, "You are not the ones to preach, sir. But if you continue, you will feel my disgust at your pathetic lies and empty threats."

He nudged the car battery with his boot toe.

Lana said, "You can't do that. He's a civilian."

The general offered mock surprise. "And you are *not*?"

Lana bit her tongue.

"Hmm," the general said as if pleased with his day's work. Then, he and his men left the cell, locking it behind them and turning off all the lights, leaving them in total darkness.

Lana called out, "How am I supposed to mediate on your

dungeon table with the lights out?"

A moment later, the kliegs clacked on, nearly blinding them. "Oh, that way," Lana said. A moment after that, the loud, tinny music cranked up again. No Zeppelin.

16

Five months passed.

Marion had been regranted all her privileges—and some peace. The press decided that either she really had not seen anything or was not going to talk about it if she had, and they left her alone. The government seemed satisfied with that arrangement, and Marion's electronics returned magically.

She woke up one morning to find her phones were back in their cradles. She had not let anyone in, not heard anyone.

Spooks, she thought. *No wonder they call them that.* "Fuckers."

Her first call was to Alanda to see how she was doing, what she might have heard. Was there any progress? Had she gotten word on Lucas's whereabouts?

Alanda told her that she was moving on and not to call again.

Then she hung up.

———

The rest of a year passed.

Marion's Marines were long gone, but little else had changed in her world. She had her routines, born out of necessity and boredom, and seldom stepped outside those self-imposed lines. She ate, read, cleaned, looked for a hobby — any distraction — and mostly ignored the news. Nothing had changed in Phnongtuk, so why bother?

Still, every day at noon, she turned on the TV at lunch and did a crossword.

This day, a reporter was updating the situation with a blue screen of the North and South divides. He said, "Though skirmishes had been going on for some time, the war officially started one year ago today and shows no sign of letting up.

"Estimates put the dead as high as a hundred-fifty-thousand or more. But no reporters have been allowed in either country since the war began, so no one knows for sure. What we do know is that this conflict is far from over, and hope has been lost by many that they will ever see their loved ones again."

Before an interview began with a stoically tearful man from Cedar Rapids, Marion switched off the television so she could finish her sandwich and puzzle in silence.

Later, Marion Cooper gathered some of Dan's old clothes and put them into boxes. As she taped one shut, she allowed her own tear to fall — and decided it would be her last.

Dan was dead. She would never see him again. It was time to let go and move on. She thought it was possible.

She had read that it was.

———————

Alanda's family celebrated her twenty-fifth birthday without her. She had said she would not attend the party and did not. Instead, she spent the evening at the Museum of Art, downtown, wandering through the vast collection, standing before the Wyeths and Hoppers, seeing nothing but Lucas's face on every figure.

Her life had ground to a halt, and there seemed nothing she could do to get it going again.

Though her mother did the best she could to try and help her daughter break through the isolation and depression, Alanda's father offered no such help. A successful entrepreneur with a thriving data analysis company, he defined himself as "a figures man." He was the reason Alanda's older brother moved to France.

"Data don't lie," was one of their father's favorites. To which Alanda nearly always replied, "Depends on the data and its source, Daddy."

When she had the energy.

Dinners with her parents were often a mix of difficult silences and more difficult conversations—if the ten words between her and her father qualified as an actual conversation—but every Sunday, they showed up at five with the victuals.

On the one-year anniversary of her return, Alanda's father appeared sterner than usual but held his tongue. Her mother saw the coming storm and tried, delicately, to intervene.

"Dear," she said to her eldest daughter, "you really need to let go of the past and return to the present. To your future."

At first, Alanda quit her job to move back home with her parents. That turned out to be misguided, and she quickly went back to her own place. Her mother kindly continued the mortgage payments while Alanda looked for a job—with little effort or results—so Alanda did not feel she could refuse their visits or their intended kindness.

"I have no future," she said with teenage bleakness and submission to her dark side as she picked at her vegan lasagna.

Her father continued to hold his tongue.

Her mother, a longtime executive assistant at the local,

family-owned chain of upscale black funeral homes, said, "It's not healthy, Allie. You need to rejoin the human race. To at least make a serious attempt at a normal life, again."

Alanda pouted. "My life will never be normal again."

"It will, dear," her mother said. "I promise."

"It won't," Alanda said, defiant and certain.

Her father could restrain himself no longer. "You need to let him go, girl."

Alanda sighed like she was twelve again. "I know, father. You warned me about him. 'No good can ever come of it,'" she parodied in her serious-father voice.

No one at the table cared to mention Lucas's race.

Alanda went on with her impression of her father, three years prior. "'He'll ruin your life.'" Then, in her own voice, "I hear that every morning, every day that I wake up alone. 'He'll ruin your life, Alanda. Mark my words.'"

Her father took the bait. "Well...."

"Oh, Daddy. Don't even," Alanda warned.

Her mother had decided to go along. "I'm afraid your father was right, dear. You have only to look at what happened."

"What happened was a war with alien spaceships attacking us on vacation!" Alanda said, her voice and ire rising. "Did you predict *that*? Did you think, 'This White boy will certainly bring aliens to earth with laser canons to ruin my daughter's life!'"

Her father ground his jaw. "I do not appreciate the gross exaggeration, Alanda. And I also do not recall mentioning his race."

"But you thought it. You implied it. And don't even try to pretend otherwise."

"I was only concerned with your wellbeing, dear," he said. Still, he could not resist adding, "But a 'surfer'? You come from a line of proud black intellectuals."

"There we go," Alanda said, pushing her chair away from the table.

Her mother stopped her. "Dear, please. Just...." Her scholarly mother was struggling with her own emotions. "Your father often chooses his words carelessly."

He bristled. She ignored him.

"All that he was trying to convey —"

"Is that I married the wrong White man. I get it," Alanda said, still standing.

Her father softened. "Alanda — my precious Alanda — it was not the color of his skin, but the color of his life."

For a reason that Alanda could not explain, this explanation hit closer to home. She sat. Her father said, "Thank you," in the most heartfelt way of which he was capable.

Then he blew it.

"There's a young man at the University, a geologist, who just received notice of tenure," he said, happily.

Alanda's jaw dropped. "Is that what this is about?"

"Now, dear," her mother said — and glared at her husband.

Alanda glared at her father as well. "You're trying to *hook me up*?"

He bristled. "I would not call it that. And I would appreciate it if —"

Alanda stood again, angry as a scalded cat.

She said, "I don't give a good goddam what you 'appreciate,' Daddy. Jesus Christ! Lucas is gone — probably dead — my *husband* whom I *loved* and *married*, despite your endless disparagements. I was delightfully *happy*! He was a wonderful man who loved me with all his heart. He was kind and decent. He loved animals. Unlike you. And he cared about me for who I am, not what he expected me to be."

Her father heard and understood her implications. He pushed back from the table. "I think it's time we go, Mother."

Alanda's mother sighed heavily. "All right, yes," she said, and stood.

No more words were said. None were needed. But as they reached the foyer, the doorbell rang. Alanda's father said back, "Are you expecting someone?"

Alanda did not care for his tone. From the dining room, she said, "I don't know, father. It is my house. Our house. My house with Lucas. Maybe it's Lucas come home."

She started for the foyer, anger roiling.

Her father opened the door before she could get to it, and she heard him say, "Yes? May I help you?"

Then Alanda saw him, Ashton Mosely—out of uniform, a bit haggard—who said only, "Sir," and nodded respectfully.

Though she was not sure why she said it, Alanda asked, "Where's your uniform?"

The brash, wild-eyed soldier who had been replaced by a hangdog, disgraced man-child said, "They threw me out for, um, well, you know. I avoided a dishonorable discharge, but they stripped my benefits. Um...."

He looked to see Alanda's father's obvious disenchantment. "Who is this person, Alanda?" he asked his daughter. "Do you know him?" He put the full weight of his position in life and the respect he expected on full display.

"Yes, I do, Daddy. His name is Ashton."

"Ashton Mosely, sir. I'm happy to meet you." He held out his hand.

Alanda's father did not accept. Further, he advised, "Close the door, Alanda. This young man obviously has the wrong house."

"Daddy!" Alanda said sharply. "Stop it." She turned to the abashed ex-soldier. "I don't understand. What did you do? Is it...what you told us?"

"Yeah," he said, with remorse. "They said I leaked confidential information."

"To *us*?"

He nodded.

"That stuff about...." She did not need to specify — or remind her father.

Ashton nodded. Stared at the ground. "There was more. It...." He looked up at her, then her father and mother. "It got even crazier before we got out of there. You were lucky to leave when you did."

"Thanks to you," Alanda said, sincerely.

Her mother had a light go on. "Is this the young soldier who helped you flee that madness?"

"Yes, mother."

"Well, come in, young man," her mother said. "Tell us what happened. You're welcome in our...our daughter's house."

"Mother," Alanda's father said, bewildered and appalled.

Ashton said, "I don't bite, sir. I promise. And I'm not insane or a bad person. I did my best under...very strange circumstances. And now I'm here and in school, trying to put my life back together." He looked down, then up at Alanda. "I, uh, I just wanted to say hello, is all. I'm sorry to intrude." He nodded and started to turn away.

Alanda's mother made her move. "You said you're in school. What are you studying? Ashton, was it?"

"Yes, ma'am," Ashton said, turning back. "Um, engineering. I was on track to become a combat engineer, when...." He sighed.

"All hell broke loose over there."

As Alanda's father continued to stare in silence, Ashton turned back to Alanda. "I'm sorry," he said. "I should go."

Alanda's mother nudged her husband. He fidgeted but relented. "No, no. You've probably come a long way. Why don't you come in, son? We were about to leave, but, uh…perhaps we should hear your story."

Alanda's mother jumped in. "Yes, please. Alanda has told us some of what happened, but it's such a wild tale! Perhaps you might enlighten us as to some specifics."

Ashton shook his head. "I'm sorry, ma'am. I've been strictly warned not to discuss anything I saw, heard, or even *think* about any of it, or they'll send me back to jail."

"Jail?" Alanda's father said, eyes widening with disapproval.

"Yes, sir, six months," Ashton said, shaking his head. "They wouldn't listen to anything I had to say or that I knew for a fact that other guys, White boys who served over there, had done the same thing. That I had a clean record, that I was confused about what I had seen and was being told. None of it. As far as I know, I'm the only one they locked up. No sir, the Army is not happy with me right now. In fact, if they even knew I was *here*, they might court-martial me just for showing up."

"They'll do nothing of the kind," Alanda's father said, and pulled Ashton inside, telling him, "I do not think highly of military *in*justice."

Ashton allowed a grin and stepped inside.

As her father closed the door behind the former sergeant, Alanda asked, "Did they…." She could not finish.

Ashton understood. "Not that I know of. No word on either your husband or Ms. Cooper's. Have you talked to her?"

Alanda flushed, guilty. "No, I...." she said. "I couldn't. The...memories. That field. The bodies." Before she knew it, she was crying, heaving, her body shaking.

Ashton reflexively took her in his arms and held her tight, bringing her almost instant relief. Then he saw her father staring — almost as wild-eyed as the locals when they saw those damned silver things fly overhead.

He pulled back. "I'm sorry," he said to her father.

Her mother assured him, "It's fine, son. What you did there is something we have been unable to accomplish for the past year."

Though Alanda did not seek more comfort from the young, disgraced man, she wiped a tear and smiled.

Her first in over a year.

17

The next time Dan awoke, he found himself attached to the table on his back with Lana strapped on top of him—both nude, scraped, bruised, bleeding—stinking of abuse and foul bodily fluids.

"Jesus," Dan said, low.

Lana's eyes opened. She lifted her head as far as the bonds would allow as she tried to focus, so close, and said, "You're awake."

"How long was I out?"

"I don't know," she said.

"You too?"

"Yeah."

Dan could feel his lower legs hanging off the end of the table, his ankles tied to the steel legs. Otherwise, he could not feel much of anything—except hunger and thirst. "They must have drugged us," he said. "I remember eating something."

"You were probably dreaming."

"Steak and lobster," he now remembered.

Lana managed a weak smile. "Ah. Not that glop they feed

us to keep us alive."

"Doesn't feel like I'm alive," he said.

"Best crash diet, ever," she said. "Captured by psychos who think you're a spy."

Dan said, "Atkins had nothing on this."

Lana stretched her neck as much as she could and reverted to what she obviously did best, avoidance and denial. "So, you come here often? What's your sign? Wanna go back to my place?"

Dan managed a half-laugh. "This is some shit we got into, huh?"

"Worse than I imagined," Lana said. "And I imagined a lot."

"They're just…it's all…." He drifted off.

Lana laid her face against his bare shoulder. "This is kind of cozy, though. At least there's that. I'd cuddle if I could move."

"This is good enough," he said.

Lana said, "Ah, but the wiles of a bound woman…."

Before Dan could try to find another chuckle, the firehose let go, all but drowning them *again* as klieg light flooded the room. With their bodies so tightly restrained, neither could do more than turn their faces away and hope the deluge stopped before they were *inadvertently* waterboarded to death.

The water stopped, locks were thrown, and the armed entourage of thugs entered around their masked leader. "Ah, the mirth. The humor. The joy!" the general said. "Laughter in the face of tragedy. A true American pastime. John Wayne!"

"Fuck off," Lana said.

"Remember what happened the last time you said that," the general warned.

"The last seven times," Lana said.

"Yes, I lose count," the general *joked*. "When I'm having

fun. Dan?"

"What she said," Dan said.

"Ah. We're getting to you. Less fire and resistance," the general said. "That is good. Good progress!"

"Fuck. You." Dan said.

"That's better," the general said, strolling closer and around them. "So, have we had time to talk? To discuss things. Maybe come up with an escape plan?"

He showed mock interest with raised eyebrows, then reached quickly towards them. His men jumped, but his hostages did not. Rather than give them credit for their steadiness under threat, he tugged at one of the ropes and said, "No, these bonds are tight and well-secured. As are you. I suppose you have begun to lose all hope of ever leaving his place, after all."

Lana barely managed enough energy — and saliva — to spit on his shoes.

"What spirit," he said. "What *joie d'vivre*." He bent closer to Dan's face. "And you?"

"Just kill me."

"I just might," the general said. "But not yet. Your usefulness has not expired."

"Then let her go," Dan said, sounding tired. "Keep me. Do whatever you want."

"That I will do, regardless. But let her go?" the general said. "No."

Dan closed his eyes. "What do you want? At least tell us that. Maybe we can make a phone call to the embassy — or an Army base. A ship."

"Quite the humorist," the general said. "But alas, all gone."

Lana said, "What do you mean?"

"Your comrades," he said. "All gone."

Lana persisted. "I don't understand."

"Of course, you don't. Your employers abandoned ship, leaving you behind on your own. No loyalty," he said, shaking his head.

"ARC is gone? Did they close the factory?" Lana asked.

"Even more of a humorist than your naked friend!" the general proclaimed with feigned delight.

Lana closed her eyes. "I'm just trying to find out if my coworkers are alive — or went back to the States. Just…. What do you mean by 'gone.'"

"I mean," The general said, leaning close, "your American might, your military, your CIA, your true friends, were ordered out of our country and left like the cowards they are, for you to suffer whatever I choose to do with you." He paused. "Until you tell the truth, and I put you out of your misery like the lying dogs you are."

Lana opened her eyes, let her deep hatred show, then tried to spit at him again. Nothing came out.

The general lit up. "Your mouth is too dry. Allow me."

He walked around, reached into a bucket, took out a ladle of water, and drank it as if it were the best thing on earth. "Our water is so pure, so clean." He held up the ladle. "Would you like some?"

He poured it on the floor.

"Maybe later, with your meal," he said, returning the ladle to its bucket. "Is the cuisine to your liking, by the way?" He put on his mock serious tone. "It is delicious, is it not? And mostly sanitary. My soldiers keep wanting to spit in it because they loath your imperialistic arrogance, but I keep warning them, 'No spitting!'" He shook his head. "As for the rest of the fluids they may be *interjecting*, I am having less good fortune, I regret."

Dan could stand no more of the man's banter. "You really are a sick fuck."

"It has been said."

"Well, they were right."

"And they are dead."

The room went quiet—until Lana sighed. "What do you want? Really?"

"What I have continued to want, the truth."

"We've told you everything," she said. "There's nothing left to say."

"Cardboard," the general said as if recalling *now*. "Vacation." He nodded.

Dan told him, "I wish I had something else to tell you. Believe me, I would flip on a dime."

"I believe that's a mixed metaphor, isn't it? 'Flip' and 'dime.' Or would that be considered a compound metaphor?"

Lana said, "They're sayings, and what they say is we don't have anything to tell you. I'm a regional support rep, and he sells tin cans."

"Copper," Dan said.

"Whatever. Metal," Lana said. "Cardboard and metal. When are you going to get that through your thick fucking greasy head!"

The general languished in the insults. "You know," he said, "you really are not very forthcoming for persons in your situation. Not to mention boldly insulting. Which leads me to believe that you do, in fact, have something to hide. Your training, perhaps—as most innocent people in your position would be begging for mercy. Not insulting me. Ah?"

"He's got a point," Dan said. The general gloated. "On the other hand," Dan went on, looking at their captor, "You're so easy."

The general's good humor vanished. "Enjoy your insolence," he said. "Everyone, even Americans — even American spies — can be broken."

"And *will*," he added, then left.

18

"Time moves more quickly than we realize," Marion said to her neighbor, Cecily Mayer.

The older woman agreed. "And the older we get, the faster it flies. Ask Norm," she said, indicating with her chin her husband, who knelt uneasily in his flower garden, weeding petunias. "Last week, he was a young stud. Now?" She shook her head.

Marion chuckled. "He's a good man," she said. "Outspoken...but a good man."

"Outspoken," Cecily repeated. "Is that code for uninformed but opinionated?"

Marion kept quiet.

"When I married him," Cecily said, "right after we got out of college, Norman was a pot-smoking hippie. Protested the war, marched for women's rights. Now?"

She looked over and shook her head again. Norman was cussing dandelions.

When Marion said no more, Cecily turned back. "How long has it been, Marion?"

"Going on sixteen months."

Cecily shook her head. "My, my," she said. "I would have said ten."

"It feels like yesterday," Marion said, woefully.

Cecily asked, "You miss him much?"

When Marion did not reply right away, Cecily looked over at Norman, who had fallen back on his ass, dumping his full weed cart all over him, and was now cussing up a storm. "I don't think I'd miss that," she said.

Marion chuckled again and said, "You know you would."

Cecily looked back at her neighbor, cocked her head, and said, "You two had some knock-down drag-outs the last year or two."

Marion felt herself blush. "You heard us?"

"Hard not to," Cecily said. "Windows open and all." She mused, "I can always tell when Norm wants to get into it. He goes around closing all the windows. Then I know the shit's about to hit the fan."

"But you've stayed together," Marion said.

"Where else I'm gonna go?" Cecily said.

Marion knew their youngest daughter LeeAnna died in her forties during a bad flu year, and their son-in-law, the husband — a die-hard liberal, according to Norman Mayer — had not spoken to them since.

Cecily once indicated that Norman's outspoken "MAGA-madness" had likely caused the rift to begin with, then sealed it when LeeAnna died from the flu. Fortunately, they had no grandkids.

Cecily said, "Cory has no room." Cory being their son, a loser in his late thirties. "Poor kid could never catch a break," Cecily said, sadly. "Alcohol didn't help, of course." She looked over at her husband, who was now angrily throwing weeds back into the hopper. "At least he stopped puttin' in his two cents all the time. Didn't seem to help much. Maybe slowed it down." Cory's impending demise.

Marion had heard that Cory lived in the basement of a married friend somewhere down in Virginia, Herndon or Sterling, as she recalled. "No room," indeed.

"Well," Cecily finally said, fidgeting as if ready to call it quits for the day. "You'll get past it, I reckon. We all do."

"I'm working on it," Marion said, honestly—then took a deep, steadying breath.

Cecily noticed. "I'm sorry, dear. That was rude of me. I've been around Norm too long. Are you okay?"

"I think so," Marion said—though she was not sure. Dan would always be in her heart, if not her life.

"What about your sister?" Cecily said. "You have a sister, right? Claudia or something? Up in Minnesota or somewheres."

"Carlie," Marion corrected. "Michigan. The U.P."

"Right," Cecily said, though it was unclear if she really remembered that part or knew where it was. "Carlie. Short for… Carlotta?"

She had read about a famous Mobster's daughter down in Miami named Carlotta something. *Murdered her father over a turf beef* is the way she remembered that episode of *Mafia Wars* on *The History Channel*.

"No, just Carlie," Marion said. "Mom and Dad had an unusual sense of humor."

"Marion's a pretty normal name."

Marion smiled. "If it wasn't the name of their favorite horse from their honeymoon."

Cecily let go of a burst of laughter filled with spit. "A *what*?" she said as Norman walked up, still muttering expletives having to do with invasive plants.

"What-what?" he said.

"Marion just told me she was named after a horse."

"A horse?" Norman laughed as if Milton Berle had been brought back from the dead to deliver the line at a roast of Don Rickles. "What *kind'*a horse?"

Cecily said, "Favorite one."

"Whose?"

"Parents?"

"Her parents?"

"Uh-huh."

"I'll be damned! A horse?" He laughed, and Cecily laughed as if Marion were not standing right next to them. Then he turned to Marion. "Why's that?"

Cecily answered for Marion. "Says they had a weird sense'a humor. Her parents."

"Well, I guess damn so!" Norman Mayer bellowed.

After the riotous mirth settled, Marion said, "Carlie and I don't speak often. We've never gotten along all that well."

Norm said, "Who's Carly?"

"Sister," Cecily said.

"Why not?" he said.

Marion did not feel the need to go into details other than, "She and Dan...had issues."

Norm said, "Well, I guess that don't matter anymore." Cecily elbowed her husband in the ribs hard enough to get a "Hey! What?"

"For Chissake, Norman. Go pick your weeds."

"Already did," he said. "You workin' on dinner or just jawbonin'?"

"I'll be in in a minute."

"That mean I should go now?"

"Does," Cecily said.

Norman gave Marion a last look—one that probably meant *You know what I mean*, and *You know that I'm right*—then he dragged his little garden wagon around the back of their house and disappeared.

"Sorry about him," Cecily said. Marion nodded. "But he's got a point," Cecily said. "Worth considerin'," she added.

Marion acceded with a half-tilt of her head.

"Well," Cecily said. "I better get dinner started, or I won't hear the end of it."

"Have to close the windows," Marion said.

"Ain't that the truth," Cecily cackled, and walked away—leaving Marion to consider what she had decided not to consider ever again.

19

Alanda opened her front door to find Ashton — with flowers.

"You called?" he said.

He looked better than the last time she had seen him six months before — filled out again, better clothes, light back in his eyes.

Alanda said, "I'm sorry it took so long. I had a lot to work through."

Ashton said, "I understand."

Feeling awkward, standing on her stoop, he held out the bouquet, which was neither lavish nor skimpy. Perfect for the situation. "These are for you," he said.

Alanda gave what the *proper* movie response. "You shouldn't have."

"I thought so," Ashton said. Then, when that sounded wrong to him, said, "I mean, I thought I should. Not that I shouldn't...have."

Alanda giggled.

"That's new," he said — and won entrance.

"Come on in," Alanda said. Then, holding the flowers in

one hand, closing the door behind them with the other, she said, "This isn't a date."

"I understand that," Ashton Mosely said, military discipline filtering into his manner.

"Okay," Alanda said. "Let me get these in a vase, then we can go."

"Okay," Ashton said, calling after her, "Did you decide what you want to see?"

Alanda said back over her shoulder on her way into the kitchen, "Anything funny."

"I'm down with that," he said, looking around the room and remembering how *not* funny his last time in this space had been. He could still feel her father's eyes burning through him as he tried to explain all that had happened—the almost-trial, gratefully avoided by his court-appointed Army defense lawyer.

In that initial, extremely uncomfortable meeting in Alanda's living room six months prior, Ashton had wanted to make it clear that a) he was not crazy, b) he was not sure *what* he had seen, and c) he was *not* allowed to talk about it ever again.

Or face Leavenworth.

Though the former Sergeant tried to hold to that, reluctant to give details, Alanda's father pressed him enough to get into the meat of his incarceration tale.

Ashton then recounted how some of the men on the transport plane home whispered rumors back and forth, confused and scared. This was not the kind of war they had signed up for. "Fucking alien shit," as they said on the big C-17.

"Battling UFOs" was the way Ashton put it to Alanda's father—unfortunately.

Her father tried to throw the disgraced young soldier out of the house three more times before he got through his story.

Alanda's mother interceded each time. "Let him tell his story, Father."

Ashton got lucky with his lawyer, he told them—after fully expecting the usual "fake-defense" approach he had heard so much about leading up to his court-martial. Everyone in the brig told him how his Army-appointed lawyer would do nothing to actually *defend* him.

"All he's gonna do," the darkest predictions came, "is maybe get you a few months off your sentence. They're all in it together. Might as well face that music and weep."

As it turned out, Captain Lawrence Dotson had a history. Or, more specifically, his father had a history—in Viet Nam.

Back in the early Seventies, at the end of that conflict, his father left their small base on patrol with a "blabbermouth cherry Louie, fresh from The Point."

How *experienced,* he thought himself.

When their platoon encountered sniper fire, the fresh West Pointer panicked, asking his seasoned sergeant for directions to the nearest outpost where they would be safe. He had heard about a secret listening post hidden deep in the jungle somewhere nearby. Did his sergeant know where it was, how to get there?

The tough-as-nails sergeant did but would not say. The listening post was secret for a reason. Giving away the location could mean giving up valuable on-the-ground intel—not to mention endangering the lives of the men there.

The young lieutenant did not see it that way and ordered his sergeant to lead them to the outpost or face court-martial for insubordination and refusing an order.

The sergeant said, "Fine," and continued to refuse as bullets continued to zing closer, returning fire in between spurns.

Ever more panicked, the green lieutenant grabbed the

phone from his radio man after the man made contact with their CC and relayed a story of imminent demise. He said they would certainly all be murdered in this ambush if he did not get directions to the forward listening base.

Despite his better judgments, the commanding officer, a nervous Captain with six days left on his short-timer stick, ordered the sergeant to lead the platoon to the secret cluster of huts. He did — and they lived.

But their rescue came with dire consequences.

When the VC figured out where the U.S. servicemen might be going, they stopped shooting. "That's a bad sign," lawyer Dotson's father Sam had said.

"No, that's a goddamn good sign," the idiot young looie said, having already pissed his pants.

And so they went. And so the location of the heretofore secret base was revealed.

Two days later, VC overran the tiny cluster of huts, and all the intel men — Green Berets, Marine Special Ops, and Linguistics specialists were killed.

As was the young lieutenant the next night — in his sleep.

When Sam Dotson got called before an inquiry commission looking into the fragging of the recent West Point grad, he had nothing to say, claiming ignorance. The tribunal officers did not believe him. Though the sergeant tried to explain the reasons the frightened-stupid lieutenant might have been low on anyone's list around the base, the Major (Asshole) on the commission sent him to jail.

In Viet Nam.

Said military prison came under mortar attack six times before the then twenty-two-year-old Sam Dotson gained release, his tour over.

The charges were ultimately dropped, but he learned a lesson, the Army needed good lawyers. Good men. Honest men. Men who could listen and make their own assessments of a situation.

He instilled this lesson in his son, young Lawrence. For though Sam, the father, had been "royally FUBAR'd by the Army," he remained a military man through and through. *His* father and his father's father both had served honorably, the former dying bravely in action.

Sam's fate was sealed before he was six. And though he gave *his* son the option of a better life and career, Lawrence heard the silent pleading and went to West Point—after earning a 4.0 in Pre-Law. In three more years, he officially became an Army lawyer, defending soldiers in trouble.

It did not go well. The new lawyer forever fought pressure from above to cut deals, to make sure his soldiers-clients did time whether he thought they deserved it or not. Most deserved what they got, but some did not.

After the tenth or twentieth, or thirtieth of those, Captain Lawrence Dotson sat in Sgt. Ashton Mosely's holding cell and listened to the most bizarre story he had ever heard and could never have imagined.

His argument before the court martial board was simple. He said, "If you were told this crazy story about aliens and UFOs and space battles in tropical jungles and ordered never to speak about it even though it was the craziest thing you had ever heard, and you had seen the awful results of whatever it was....

"What would you do, sirs? I ask only that you be honest in your silent responses and show a merciful understanding for this young, frightened, very confused young soldier who had until he spoke about the horrors he saw because he could no longer keep it inside without going crazy and killing himself—for he considered that every day, every hour — who had served bravely, fiercely, and loyally for five years, never questioning an order, never getting written up for so much as a cigarette butt out of place…I ask you…for lenience."

It worked.

Ashton got his discharge—not dishonorable, but he had to give up all benefits. And he had to agree never to speak of those strange occurrences again—true or not.

He agreed and shared what else he could of his story to Alanda, her mother, and her father six months earlier in the living room where he now stood, waiting for his non-date to come back from watering her bouquet.

"They're lovely, Ashton," Alanda said as she returned to put the modest bouquet on her mantel. "Shall we?"

"We shall," Ashton said, grinning.

————

The movie was not great, but it was funny—just what they both needed.

"I haven't laughed like that since I was a kid," Ashton told Alanda as they walked back out through the lobby of the multiplex.

"Me neither, I think," she said. "At least not in the last year."

"I had no idea he was such a good actor."

"Me either," Alanda agreed. "Or her!"

"Yeah, who knew?"

"I wish I had her body," Alanda said. "That pool scene? Wow."

"Are you kidding me?"

"What?"

"You're way hotter."

"Stop."

Ashton halted abruptly.

Alanda was three steps ahead when she realized and turned back. "What?"

"You said 'stop,'" he said.

"Oh!"

Alanda made a mock production of going back to get Ashton moving again, shoving him ahead like a female Sisyphus, Ashton pretending to resist.

Both laughing like teenagers on a first date — the release they both needed.

20

News of the warring countries eventually gave way to more pressing matters at home. The new president stayed in a constant war with Congress over budgets and Canadian dairy products while small conflagrations popped up all around the globe. As always, American troops were the center of global policing, causing protests the world over — instability the new norm.

Marion stopped watching the news when reporting of the earthquake numbers fell off. The final tally came in at somewhere near 160,000, with 120,000 more lost to war — though those numbers could not be confirmed. It could have been double, some said — or half. No one knew.

Reports occasionally popped up regarding the ongoing questions surrounding the initial attacks, but since no new information had been provided by either side, the media focused on other ledes.

Don Lemon went to Estonia.

On the eighteen-month anniversary of coming home alone, Marion made the difficult decision to officially move on. In one long day, starting before dawn, she packed the rest of Dan's things—clothes, sports gear, and personal items—and sealed them in more boxes. Late that afternoon, she watched as the Goodwill truck pulled up, and two men in used clothes loaded it all into the back of their van, shut the door, and drove away.

The day had been long and taken it out of Marion Cooper. She cried empty tears as she closed the front curtains and did not sleep that night.

The next day, Marion felt even more fatigued—tired from not sleeping but mainly worn out from life and its endless exigencies. She told herself she was merely embarking on "a new chapter" but could not bring herself to accept or even believe the concept. Certainly not to embrace the notion of finality.

Turning that new first page seemed unimaginable.

Though Marion Ansley-Cooper was world-wise enough to know that life rarely goes the way we expect, she was also educated enough to know that no one in their right mind could ever have predicted all that she had been through—and that included anything from the four-and-a-half decades that preceded the Phnongtuk tragedies.

Seeing her nephew, a toddler, killed by a car, and her other sister, the mother, committing suicide a week later. Her parents dying. Dan's parents dying. Cancer, heart attacks, liver failure, more accidents—all of it awful, yet nothing came close to the madness in Phnongtuk.

But that chapter had ended, Marion told herself. Now, things would be different. They would have to be. And so, Marion Cooper embarked on a new chapter.

Like it or not.

To begin, Marion knew she would have to reintroduce herself to old friends, her long-abandoned writing group, maybe join some other groups—say, gardening or doily making. *Jesus,* she thought. *I'm not* that *old.* A rare smile crossed her face.

Maybe she could get involved in politics—making calls, canvassing, wearing buttons. Take on some DIY projects. Build a fence around the house to protect her private moments and keep out the rest of the world.

That all felt too ambitious. Repainting the dining room seemed a better place to start. Not too demanding, not a critical change, nothing that would unintentionally disrespect her past with....

Dan is gone. She had to remind herself several times a day. *Not coming back.*

Since Marion had chosen the previous color for the dining room, "That's perfect," she decided. It would not be like undoing something he, or they, had chosen.

The trip to Benjamin Moore proved more demanding and less fun than she had imagined. The man behind the counter seemed new—or disinterested—and suggested that choosing a color or finish was not his prerogative.

Marion went to Lowes. *Is everyone in the county here?* she wondered.

After a long hour of waiting her turn, getting much better advice from a tattooed young girl with an asymmetrical hairdo, Marion chose a "slightly vibrant spring blush green" on the girl's suggestion—in eggshell, for the dining room. "I always recommend semi-gloss or at least eggshell for rooms with food," the girl said.

Marion could not remember whether her walls at home were "somewhat shiny or kind of flat," so she accepted the advice, chose semi-gloss, and walked around to kill the thirty minutes the girl would need to get Marion's paint mixed and ready, given the other orders ahead of her.

Keeping a constant eye on her watch, Marion perused bathroom fixtures—comfort-height toilets and glass above-counter sinks—deciding the old ones were fine. She considered new blinds but could not make up her mind between wide and mid-wide, white or "natural wood look."

She moved over one aisle to leaf through pre-sized room rugs—"Oriental" and modern—ran her fingers over floor laminates and tiles and took a quick look at kitchen cabinets. The pushy salesman made her want to blast him with an alien laser, so she went back to the paint counter early.

"Sorry, it's gonna be another twenty," the girl said, rushing cans of freshly colored paint to impatient homeowners and one testy overall-wearing painter who kept tapping his watch.

"Okay," Marion said, and headed out to the Garden Center, where she considered roses, forsythia, and viburnum. But since she still did not feel a hundred percent, she passed on all but a small potted geranium—just because—and went back to wait in line to await her paint.

Next came Harris Teeter—"Hairless Peter," Dan always called it. Not one of his better lines, Marion always thought. Now, she kind of missed his corny jokes.

Stop! she told herself. *Move on.*

Marion's shopping list was not long but detailed. She had had a hankering for pot roast after poring over the weekly flyer—something she had never done in her past life—and looked for the sale.

Two left.

Feeling lucky, if not perky, Marion gathered the other items on her list—some 85% cocoa bars (*Perfectly bitter*), "Hi-Proteen" pasta (*Why the hell can't they just spell it properly?*), tomatoes that looked red enough but probably had no more taste than the green ones (*I'm not frying the damn things*), and an upscale brand of instant pudding. (*Isn't all pudding in a box 'instant'?*).

At least she had not lost her sense of outrage at the trivial.

Further thinking on the tomatoes almost sent Marion back to Lowes for some tomato plants so that she could at least have some real ones with flavor before fall came, but she opted to head home and put her roast in the oven so that she could enjoy it with her favorite classical music program on her local NPR station that started at seven p.m.

She did make sure to pick up a nice bottle of Merlot.

Driving alone had felt strange at first — which was strange because Marion was often on her own when Dan went out of town on business or worked at the office. But knowing he would not be coming home — ever — made her driving experience uncomfortable and lonely. Though she felt a welling in her chest, she forced it away.

A close call at a stoplight helped. Apparently, the red runner didn't even see her.

Inches.

Walking through the kitchen door in back brought on a deep sigh, Marion both exhausted and happy to be home. This had not been her longest excursion out since coming back, but it seemed that way. Putting away the groceries felt as lonely as driving.

The geranium looked small and singular on the back portico. Insignificant. Assessing its tiny stature and lack of enhancing effect, Marion wondered if she would forget to water it, ignoring it to death as she had all the houseplants over the years, so she transplanted it into a larger pot and soaked the soil until it could take no more moisture.

"Hmmph," she said of *all that work* and went back inside

to prepare the roast and stick it in the oven.

A glass of wine and re-reading a few chapters of "P is for Peril," took some of the edge off—sitting in the waning warmth of the lowering sun didn't hurt—but Marion could not shake her fatigue. She let the book drop into her lap and closed her eyes, dreaming of dreaming the coming night away, but rest did not come.

When the oven beeped, Marion realized she was not hungry after all. The roast smelled good—rosemary did that to her—but the thought of eating more than a few bites had no appeal.

She stood back when opening the oven door to allow the steam to flow out around her and keep her reading glasses from steaming up. Then with oven-mitted hands, she reached in for the heavy roast, thinking, *How am I ever going to eat all this? It will last a month or*—

The thought was not fully out of her mind as she stood up with the odorous large Pyrex baking dish, and it simply fell out of her hands, crashing onto the floor, sending meat, juices, potatoes and carrots skittering across the hardwood floor.

————

Marion awakened in a single room at the Shady Oak Grove hospital, flanked by Cecily and Norman Mayer on one side and a young Pakistani doctor on the other. She quickly closed her eyes before anyone noticed they had fluttered open for a moment.

Norman saying, "Dumb luck, the missus went over."

"Something didn't feel right," Cecily said.

"She has notions," her husband said.

"I sense things," she said.

"A real Uri Gellar she is, sometimes, I tell you. It's spooky."

Cecily took his hand in hers. Seeing their much-younger

neighbor in a hospital bed, attached to wires and tubes, hopefully soon to regain consciousness had its effect.

The doctor—his name tag read Khudiadadzai, but everyone called him Doctor K—said, "Well, whatever drove you to check on her was a lucky thing. Mrs. Cooper had a seizure. We're not sure why yet, but we're running every test known to mankind." He smiled with the confident reassurance that only doctors can muster.

"What brought it on?" Norman asked, getting a new elbow from his wife, who apparently did not feel that was any of their business. He shrugged as if to say, *What? I just wondered. Don't you want to know? It's not every day someone as young as Marion has a seizure for no reason.*

All in one look.

Dr. K said, "We believe it might be a delayed response to an earlier concussion she received while out of the country."

"Oh," Mrs. Mayer said. "*There.*" That single word carried as much odiousness as her husband's earlier shrug.

Dr. K leafed through her file. "Apparently, she saw another doctor here about headaches a few months back, and they noted that she had suffered a rather severe concussion while on vacation last year."

"Yessss," Cecily Mayer said, another single word laden with portent and realization.

"Will she be okay?" Norman asked.

"We believe so. In time," the doctor said. "We have a choice of medications and therapies available. The main thing is to observe her closely and regularly, get the results back and... we'll see. I'm optimistic." He smiled and, after glancing at his paperwork, asked sensitively—probably so as not to offend the older couple, "Does she have any family?

Norm said, *sans* sensitivity, "No, she's alone. Her husband was killed on that vacation. Drowned or swept away or something."

The doctor looked up, not understanding.

Mrs. Mayer helped him out. "In that big earthquake over there, in what's-it-called, before that war started. You know, over there in...."

She looked at Norm, who shrugged. Damned if he could remember.

The doctor did. "Ah yes, that's right. Phnongtuk. I do recall seeing that in the file. That was quite an event."

While he looked for the reference in the file, Norman Mayer added, "They said on television it may have been space people. Aliens. I call bullshit on that."

"Norman," Cecily said sharply.

"It's true!" he said.

"I believe I recall something of that order as well," the doctor said with studied impartiality. Hard to tell if he had heard it or not. Probably just did not want to get into it. "So, you were saying."

They looked at him blankly.

"Her family? Anyone other than her husband who is deceased."

"Sister in Minneapolis," Norman said.

"Michigan," his wife said. "Pediatrician, I think."

"I thought you said veterinarian," he said.

"Some kind of doctor," she said.

"Vet ain't a doctor. It's animals," he said.

"Still a doctor," Cecily said. "Just for animals."

"That's what I said."

Dr. K had heard enough to move on with his questioning,

"Do you have a way to contact her — the sister?"

Cecily said, "I may have her number, or I can get it from Marion's house. We have a key."

"Good," the doctor said, removing a card from his pocket. "If you find it, give my office a call. She's going to need some help for a few weeks at least."

Cecily took the card and read over it with interest and doubt. "How do you pronounce that?"

"Just call me Doctor K. It's easier on all of us." He gave his physician smile and turned to go.

Norman asked, "Does she have insurance?"

Cecily elbowed him harder than the last three times and got the same shrugging silent sentence.

"Yes," Dr. K said. "On her husband's policy." He looked at the pages but decided not to offer any personal details. "It's actually...yes," he said and left.

Norman grunted. "But he's dead."

Cecily grunted along. "Must've been good insurance from that hardware store company. Better'n any you ever got with the airline."

"Bastards," was all Norm had to say about that.

They took a final full assessment of Marion, her eyes still closed — assuming she was out cold — and Norman said, "You think she'll wake up ever?"

"I don't know," Cecily said. "But we best go try and find her sister's phone number. I've got the key, you know."

"Of course, I know. You just said it," Norm groused.

"Oh, hush," his wife said. And they argued all the way out into the parking lot and home.

Awake, eyes closed, Marion had heard every word of caution, hope, and despair. Could this damn thing, this life of hers, get any worse?

She dared herself to think it. Somehow, that gave her the courage to continue.

21

The next time Alanda opened the door for Ashton Mosely, she was dressed and ready to go to lunch. Dinner had been offered, but lunch seemed safer.

The light of day.

This time, she chose one of her favorite little bistros on a small lake with six tables outside to enjoy the view. Since the day was nippy, she and Ashton had the place to themselves after the noon rush.

"Pretty," he said, taking in the colorful reflections off the still lake — more to fill a conversation void than comment on the location.

"Lucas and I used to come here when the weather was nice," Alanda said.

Ashton smiled politely but said nothing.

"So," Alanda said after the server had taken their soup and sandwich orders, "what was jail like? I can't imagine."

"It was hell," Ashton said.

Alanda repeated her inability to conceive of such, and Ashton said, "But not like you'd think. Not like on TV."

"Oh," Alanda said, no doubt having imagined riots and burning mattresses in a two-tiered prison bloc.

"Military confinement is...stricter," he said. "No rapes, no protests, no throwing poop at the guards."

Alanda laughed.

"So much protocol," he said. "Endless protocols. No visitation. Your lawyer almost never checks in on you."

"But you said he was good."

"He was, he was," Ashton said. "But he had a lot of other cases, and they only allow so much contact unless there is an impending hearing or something; and, since we were essentially done—that's how the Army does things—he had no reason to visit. So he didn't."

Ashton reconsidered that statement. "Well, he did. More than the others—than the other inmates got. But just to tell me nothing had changed and ask if I was doing okay. If I needed anything."

"That was nice," Alanda said. "I suppose."

"Oh yeah," Ashton said. "I just...I never needed anything. And nothing changed."

"Was it clean?" she wondered.

"Oh yeah. They make sure of that," he told her. "We have to keep our cells as spotless as our bunks in basic."

"Scrubbing toilets with a toothbrush?" she joked.

"Well, yes—but without the toothbrush. That's kind of a myth," he said.

"I thought so," Alanda said, demurely—as if she felt foolish.

Ashton took her hand. "You're doing fine," he said.

Alanda looked up. "Am I? I don't feel like I am."

"I think you're doing incredible," he said.

Alanda smiled — and retrieved her hand. "So…what else happened?"

"Oh," he said, sighing — not seeming to worry about the loss of physical contact — "the usual. Lots of mental abuse. Calling us names. 'Traitor' and the like."

Alanda was shocked. "You weren't a traitor!"

"No, but those guards are hardcore," he said. "They figure if you're in military jail, you screwed the pooch and can't be trusted."

"That's awful," she said. "What's 'screw the pooch'?"

"Fucking up royally."

"Oh. Still," she said.

He shrugged it off. "They're trained that way. *Picked* to be that way." He threw his head around. "The 'best of the best!'"

"Sounds like the worst of the worst," she said in his defense.

"It gets to you," he said. "I won't deny that. Having your fellow soldiers call you names without having any idea what you went through. It's…it was disheartening."

"What else did they say?"

"It doesn't matter," he said. "They did what they were trained to do. Believed what they were told to believe. Just like us all. That's the Army."

"I don't think I'd like the Army," she said.

Ashton laughed. "Yeah," he said. "I don't think so."

As their food arrived, Alanda perked up. "My favorite," she said of the white chowder and grilled Brie with heritage tomatoes and braised cilantro.

Ashton had told the waiter he would have what Alanda was having and now wondered if he had been correct. But one sip of the soup and a cautious bite of the sandwich, and he was elated. "Wow," he said. "This really is good."

"Better than what you got in prison, I bet," she said, apparently happy to be eating and moving on.

"Actually," Ashton told her, "the food wasn't bad. Not like this, but it was pretty good, considering. And they had decent cable. And we got to use the gym. Play basketball every day. It wasn't that bad, accommodations-wise."

"Just the guards," she said.

"Well," he said, "the groveling, mainly."

"What do you mean?" Alanda said, wiping the corner of her mouth daintily.

A detail Ashton could not help but notice.

"All the fake 'yessir's and the phony respect I had to show because they'd all been told I was a traitor."

"But you weren't," Alanda protested.

"They didn't know that," Ashton said in their defense. "Anyway, it wasn't a fun six months, I can tell you that. But it could have been a lot worse." He gazed at a happy White couple in a paddleboat, sipping white wine and laughing their way past, waving at anyone who would notice them.

Ashton waved and told Alanda, "There were times I thought they didn't believe any of what they had been told. You know, I was just a grunt-made-sergeant, doing what I was told."

"Like them."

"Exactly." Ashton stared this time at nothing. "Then, one day, a new lawyer showed up."

"Oh no," Alanda said.

"No, it was cool," Ashton told her. "He came into my cell, told me it was all over, and I was being released—no DD but no benefits. No college or VA or anything."

"But you didn't do anything wrong," Alanda said.

Ashton was not so sure. "I shouldn't have told what I did," he said and looked away, feeling the weight of that decision. "It's weird, but...."

Alanda smiled softly and touched his hand, this time. "You felt a connection, too."

Ashton looked down at her hand on his and said, "I wasn't going to say that."

Though he was not harsh in his tone, Alanda retrieved her hand. "I'm sorry. I shouldn't presume."

"No, no," Ashton said. "It's not that. I didn't mean that."

"What?" she said, less warmly.

As he waved at the paddleboat couple passing again — still laughing, probably half-drunk, he reckoned — he said, "It's like...I don't know. Like they *wanted* me to tell you."

That caught Alanda by surprise. "What do you mean 'wanted'? Who?"

"My commanding officers," he said and lowered his voice. "It was weird, Alanda. They called this meeting. We had this meeting. There were maybe...thirty of us."

"Soldiers?"

"Non-coms. Sergeants like me. A few corporals," he said. "I didn't know it at the time, but all of us had been assigned to certain tourists."

Alanda stopped eating. "Like us? Lucas and me?"

"Actually, Dan and Marion," Ashton said. "You were just...there."

"Oh," Alanda said, sounding let down.

"No," he said. "I mean, you were *there*. It was like the whole thing changed. I...." He took her had hand fully in his. "I fell in love the instant I saw you, Alanda. I've never felt anything like that before. It was like my whole life changed in that moment.

The instant I saw you. It was like…whoosh, I was swept away."

Alanda looked at his hand, then away — then retrieved hers.

"I'm sorry," Ashton said immediately. "That as…I didn't mean to—"

"No," Alanda said, not looking at him. "It's okay. I understand."

As Ashton stumbled around his interior world, groping for where to go next, Alanda said, quietly, "Go on. About the meeting."

Ashton said, "No. You're married. That was wrong of me."

"Wrong?" she said.

"Wrong for me to feel that," he said. "Marriage is sacred. It's…what do they say? Inviolable. At least it is for me."

Alanda stared deeply.

Ashton said, "But I knew I could do something for you. I could help."

"With the flight out."

"Yes. And with…information."

"About the aliens and stuff," she confirmed for him. "I don't think I believe that anymore," she said. "Do you?"

Ashton did not answer her question directly. He said, "All I know is, in that meeting, they told us all about it. Everything I told you. And they said, 'Keep this close. Only discuss it with those you trust.'"

"That *is* weird," Alanda agreed.

Ashton said, "We all looked around at each other, all of us non-coms, and I think we all realized at the same moment that we had never seen each other before. We were all busy with our assigned victims. You know, everyone else was on patrol or guard duty or helping the engineers with cleanup and body removals, that kind of thing. But all of us in that tent, we were on a different assignment. To deal with specific American tourists — just the ones we were given. I mean, we had all been ordered not to talk to anyone else except 'in the pursuit of assistance' with those specific Americans. That's what they told us."

He could still hear the words being said as if their waiter had said them a moment earlier.

Ashton looked directly at Alanda — as if searching for an answer — and said, "So who were we gonna tell?"

He raised a good question. One for which Alanda had a singular insight, "You logically inferred that it was okay to tell us."

"Right," Ashton said, reenergized. "You were the only people I saw. Had contact with except for my Commanding Officer, Captain Wainwright, who kept me running day and night, keeping up with the other six couples he gave me. I only got to sleep maybe two hours a night. I was fucking exhausted. Like a zombie. I went back and forth between you and them and...."

He shook his head, feeling that overpowering fatigue and stress again.

Alanda wondered, "Did you tell them, too?"

"No," Ashton said. "Just you guys. You and Marion."

"Why not the others?" Alanda asked.

"I don't know," he said. "Just a feeling, I guess."

"You trusted us," Alanda said.

"I guess so," he said. "We didn't...connect, I guess. Like with you."

Alanda said, "You looked so scared that day."

"I was," Ashton said with no embarrassment. "I was freaked out. I mean, *aliens*? Come on. Laser beams, space warfare?

Then they said not to discuss it with anyone. Just people we 'could trust.' Who would that be? None of us knew each other. Just that was weird enough. Not one of us had gone through basic together or served anywhere together. It was like they brought together this team that wasn't a team, that didn't know each other, and warned us not to discuss what we were being told...."

Ashton shook his head. "I was confused as hell, just like every other man in that tent. And they were all men, by the way. I don't know what that means."

Alanda had an opinion, "Men are more likely to follow orders without questioning."

Ashton looked sharply. "I wouldn't say that."

"Think about it," she said.

Ashton did, then sheepishly nodded, not sure that he *wanted* to think about it. Then he said, "Anyway, there we were. It was a living conundrum." He scoffed. "Pretty much like the whole damn military."

"Then they arrested you for it."

"And threw me in jail," he said. "Fucking military."

Alanda let the moment float away as they returned to the final bites of their lunch—Ashton opting not to eat further, distressed.

Finally, Alanda said, "They said on TV it might be true."

"I don't watch TV anymore," Ashton said.

"Me neither," Alanda confessed. "Now."

After a moment, Ashton's features turned darker. "You know he's not coming back, right?"

Alanda bit her lip and let go of Ashton's hand.

22

In the North, it came time for another show of power.

A gaggle of men with cameras shuffled into place by a large hangar on what appeared to be an air base—though no planes were visible. A set of four rails set in the tarmac led away from the hangar—two sets of tracks spread wide. A single, smallish mountain poked up in the near-distance, pointy and cragged. Otherwise, the surrounding land was mostly flat as befits an airbase.

While men and women, apparently technicians, scurried here and there—most of them in white radiation suits—a military *cortège* walked solemnly toward a plain stage equipped with a podium and, incongruously, several large tropical floral sprays.

Lesser officers herded the potential recorders of this event—the "reporters"—to a cordoned-off space mostly in front of the platform, affording them a view of the podium, the hangar, and the mountain.

Carefully staged.

Amid the thirty or more high-ranking military officials stood a multiple-star general, short in stature. He paid little attention to the "press," his sycophantic officers corps, or the flowers. He did check on the closed doors of the hangar and took a moment to appreciate the panorama.

When an order passed up through the ranks, the general nodded casually, whispered something to his attaché, and took the dais to speak, maybe into the camera, maybe not.

Had Dan and Lana had access to a television, they would have recognized the voice, if not the face, of their dehumanizing general.

He said, "We are here to address the many lies being reported by foreign media that we do not possess superweapons. We do. And we will give a small demonstration of the power and accuracy of these weapons. What you are about to witness will be like nothing you have ever witnessed in your lives. What you will see is a revelation, a harbinger of things to come, and a clear warning to those who would stand in our way."

The general looked to his subordinates, some with enough fruit salad on their uniforms to open a Dole factory. All nodded on cue.

"Let me be clear," he said in his calm voice, "these are the most powerful superweapons the world has ever known. Though these paid liars of the international fake news cabal feel free to question our legitimacy, the legitimacy of our war effort and its certain outcome, as well as the legitimacy of our very form of government itself, no longer will they be able to deny our military capabilities—on any scale."

The general turned away to watch as the two enormous hangar doors slid open, revealing only dark shadows inside— more people in white suits hurrying about—then he turned back with a smile to continue into his small array of mics.

Hard to tell how many were plugged in.

"We will demonstrate," he said, "on a very small scale, the minimal capabilities of our weaponry — one in particular — designed for us and by us with assistance from, shall we say, universal intelligence."

Though it seemed doubtful that many there spoke English, when the general laughed, his sycophantic cabinet joined him, sharing looks of confidence and joy, nodding to each other to show their enthusiasm for coming uses of these weapons.

Happy annihilations.

The general smiled and nodded appreciation, then turned to watch with the others as a titanic *machine* the size of two railcars joined together with two more stacked on top appeared on the tracks, propelled from its hiding place with silent motors.

The crowd gave a unison gasp, for this device did *not* look like anything anyone had ever seen before — unless in a Buck Rogers movie of old. Was it a gun? There was no barrel. Was it a vessel? A boxy spaceship? A building on rails?

Whatever, the giant thing appeared to be metal — a massive box some two stories high, adorned with protrusions here and there — boxes on boxes, things on things. On the closest side hung a glassed-in cubicle that had not one but three fixed seats for the operators, presumably, and three panels of controls surrounding the seats like a next-generation Airbus cockpit.

Many glowing.

The front of the big white box was adorned with a raised, articulated circular object that looked like a large lens, a giant purple eye. As the beastly cyclopic thing made its way toward its destination point at the end of the rails, the lens extended out, pivoted, tilted, and rotated as if running an internal test, finally coming to rest facing forward and angled slightly upwards — all without the apparent aid of an operator.

The general turned back to his A-camera. "Our machine will be able to send a beam of energy anywhere in the world that we choose. At this time, our range is limited to 1400 miles — that is to say, roughly twenty kilometers past our enemy's furthest border." He smiled again, contented and proud.

"But in the very near future, within mere weeks, we will have extended that range by two, then by four, and then by eight — a total of roughly 12,000 miles, or almost precisely halfway around the globe in any direction."

The assembled crowd "Oooo'd" and "Ahhhh'd," scribbling notes as cameramen took up new positions in what appeared to be a carefully-orchestrated show.

"Yes," the general said, agreeing with the moans regarding the magnificence of his predictive oratory as the colossal rolling block of a thing reached the end of its tracks and stopped, rocking a bit as it settled — either massively heavy or whimsically flimsy.

The general made one last turn back to watch as three of his suited technicians climbed into the cockpit, sat, strapped in, put on protective eyeglasses, and began going through furious "pre-launch protocols," throwing switches, pushing buttons, checking meters, and causing multiple banks of lights to become active.

Many turned red.

As the technician in the middle took hold of a control yoke — a combination of airplane controls, space station esoterica, and good old-fashioned Caterpillar-style skid-steer applications — the tech closest to the closest window looked out and gave a thumbs-up as if to say, *Locked and loaded, Sir!*

The general saluted, turned back to his crowd, and said, simply, "Observe."

A wailing siren warned to "stand clear," and everyone

near moved away. Some of the reporters cowered back. The general stood erect, expectant.

A beeper "counted down" — sounding like a garbage truck backing up — and red lights swung this way and that, warning of impending dangerous action. Finally, a loud, sharp buzz was heard, and the lens on the front glowed bright purple, then — nothing.

For three seconds.

Everyone looked to their left — cued by the camera operators and their lenses — and a moment later, the top of the mountain exploded violently. A blast that appeared as large and effective as a volcanic eruption took off the entire peak. Fire and brimstone launched hundreds of feet into the air in a cloud of flames and smoke.

The assembled went agog with surprise and awe, which appeared genuine. Everything appeared real — frighteningly real.

Especially the vile glee on the general's face.

He then looked up as, seconds later, three of the oddly shaped silver objects roared overhead so fast and low it seemed they were gone before they arrived.

That now familiar shrill, shrieking *otherworldly* scream.

"That," the general said, turning back to his main camera, "is a warning. As clear as any warning has ever been. Do not attempt to interfere in our reunification efforts — our 'war' if you like. This is our country's business. And neither the South, nor any of our neighbors, nor any power or *claimed* superpower on the globe is safe. Any attempt to intercede in our efforts will be met with this greater power — a power *so* great that no one has ever seen nor could ever imagine. A power that comes from the very core of the galaxy itself — and beyond. A power that only we possess, and that we will use, without discretion, on any persons, military, or *country* that attempts in any way to invalidate our goals of achieving total surrender from our obstinate brothers and sisters to the south." He looked down as if he sensed the camera zooming in on his face.

"We will destroy you," he said directly into the camera.

With that, he gave a hubristic wave of his hand, and the giant machine began its slow roll back into the hangar. Though the demonstration was over, debris would continue to fall for an hour — all of which had been broadcast to the world.

The world noticed.

———————

No one noticed more than the new president of the South, who had watched the broadcast from his imperial palace with his own somber cabinet and military leaders. When the grand chandeliers rattled above their heads, their president lost his shit.

"This calls for retaliation of an extraordinary nature. Announce that we are willing to do whatever we must take whatever steps are available to us, and use any and all forms of weaponry to combat this supernaturalistic attack on our sovereign soil. We shall prevail!"

He angrily slapped off the broadcast and gave his new standing order, "Attack!"

23

Late-night comedians had a different reaction to the international broadcast.

Billy Patterson, a Bill Maher replacement clone, put it to his three guests this way, "Come on, seriously? All they had to do was put a big bomb on top of that mountain and time it to blow up when the guy from *Dr. No* pushed the button."

His guests and audience got the joke, so he rode that comedy wind. "I mean, I've seen bad movies that did it better. Remember the exploding wagon in *Von Helsing*? Anyone?" After allowing a gap for applause, he finished with, "The only thing missing was Mike Meyers' cat in the lap."

One of his guests, a former congressman known for his fundamentalist conservative views, said, "Bill, I understand you're an atheist and a cynic, but bigger things *are* possible in this world."

He smiled, so Patterson refrained from shredding him and went with typical sarcasm. "So, you're saying you believe these banana republicans—"

He held for audience response.

"These two-bit military dictator types blew up a mountain with a giant laser machine built by aliens. Is that what you're saying?"

"I'm saying," his guest said, "we don't know."

"Oh, I think we know," Patterson said. "And by the way, that is the stupidest reason to believe something." He put on his Maher-like mocking voice. "'We can't prove it isn't true, so we will prance along our way not *dis*believing it.'"

Then, on to his copied breaking point of being pushed past humor. "That's pathetic and stupid."

His guest, a regular, was not fazed. "I'm just saying we can't be certain that it was faked, and we should be open to any possibility. We'd be foolish to cast if off without closer examination."

Patterson shot back, "And I'm saying the laser machine in that *Pink Panther* movie that cut Clouseau in half was more believable than that fucking thing."

The audience roared, so he looked at them and asked, "Do you remember that stupid thing? Tell me this didn't look exactly like that. They probably have that movie on VHS and have been hitting rewind for months to get it just right."

He mimicked pointing a remote at a VCR and stabbing at the pause button, bringing riotous applause.

His hyper-conservative guest held firm. "I don't think we can judge this demonstration by a silly movie. I think we need to consider the power and scope, the potential of this weapon — and possibly fear it."

The audience gave a resounding, facetious "*Oooooooo*" to that notion.

Prepared for the reaction, Patterson grinned. "Well, in honor of your theory, we have parting gifts for my guests."

At that, one of his staff brought out pre-formed tinfoil hats for everyone on the panel, all of whom put them on — Patterson included — except for the designated denier.

The audience loving it all.

"Oh, come on," Patterson said to him. "It's a comedy show. Wear the damn thing. You'll be surprised at how much fun it is to get laughs instead of groans." With that, Billy Patterson stood up, moved over, and put the tin cone on the guest's head.

The audience cheered.

"See?" Patterson said as he returned to his chair. "It's nice to be liked."

Applause mixed with laughter as Patterson looked into the camera, tinfoil hat affixed, and said, "New rule, If you blow up a mountain and say 'Aliens did it,' you better have a fucking alien on hand to confirm it."

The rest of the late-night shows took similar approaches. Only the White House kept quiet.

———

In her hospital bed, Marion Cooper wanted to laugh but could not bring herself to it. The next morning, she was going home.

When daylight broke, nurses came into her room, feeding her breakfast, being cheerful about her "recovery."

Six hours later, as is the way with hospital departures, Marion sat in a wheelchair pushed by a nurse to a Honda CRV outside the exit doors as Carlie parked her older sister's car and got out to help her into the front seat.

"The keys were where I told you?" Marion said.

"Yes, Mare. Right where you told me," Carlie said. "Last week." She then looked at the nurse. "She was a handful, I'm guessing."

The nurse rolled her eyes good-naturedly and said, "She

was fine." But she made a quick getaway back inside before Marion could *comment*.

Carlie looked down at her sister. "You are the worst patient ever. Always have been."

"Take me home," was all Marion gave in response as she rose out of the wheelchair and swayed slightly.

"Easy," her sister ordered.

Marion yanked away and helped herself into the car. "They don't even know what's wrong with me. Probably just low blood sugar. I got light-headed from not eating all day."

Carlie sighed. "You had a seizure, Marion. You were still flopping around on the floor when your neighbor found you."

"Cecily Mayer?" Marion said, scoffing. "You can't trust anything she says. Her husband's worse."

Carlie stopped short. "Marion, what has happened to you? Are you going to start standing out on your porch yelling at kids to get off your lawn, next?"

Marion turned to her sister, straight on. "Carlie, I appreciate you being here. I do. But you can go home now."

"No way," Carlie said, closing the door and going around to drive. Getting in, she said, "I'm not going anywhere until we're certain it isn't going to happen again."

Before the CRV was moving, Marion told her, "How can we ever be 'certain' of that? Shit happens, Carlie. Shit happens that is so out of our control we can't even begin to grasp what it is or what it means."

Marion looked out the window at the hospital, calculating which room on the second floor had been hers. "Or what will happen next."

Memories of Phnongtuk had made Marion Cooper not trust in any future.

Carlie heard the fear in her sister's voice. "Well, let's get you home, see that you're settled—"

"Then you can go back to Marquette," Marion said. "I don't need your help."

Carlie drove the rest of the way without comment.

That evening, Marion insisted on cooking dinner. They ate in silence, only the sounds of forks on china. Later, Marion would not let Carlie touch a plate; she washed everything—avoiding the dishwasher—then dried and put everything away.

Just to prove she could—on a cane.

Before bedtime, Marion swallowed the two pills she had been prescribed—under Carlie's direct supervision. "I know how to take pills," Marion told her younger sister.

Carlie said, "I'm not here to instruct."

Marion said, "Good," and tucked herself in. Though she tried to stay focused, reading a book on the region they had chosen to vacation in, trying to understand what in hell's name had really happened, Marion's eyes got heavy quickly, and before she knew it, she was snoring.

Carlie came in to put the book on Marion's nightstand with her reading glasses and stared at her older sister for several minutes before turning out the light.

Then she went to the guest room to pack.

24

Photos and videos of the strange "laser explosion" machine covered the internet. It was now being referred to as the Tesla-izer, after the inventor's concept of a machine that could shoot energy through the planet and blow up something on the other side of the world.

Twitter had fun with it—until wider shots emerged, revealing...something.

In the hangar shots, the huge machine itself sat inert, nonthreatening, but behind it, in soft focus, lay two large, rounded objects mostly covered in tarps. Just enough oddly contoured metal showed to draw speculation as to possibly otherworldly origins. Open-source analysts pored over the pics, noting that, oddly, the machines sat unguarded. But they had no explanations as they had indeed never seen anything like it.

Any of it.

In the South, a surge attack was mounted. Columns of soldiers in tanks and other armed vehicles swept northward. Jets flew overhead, and naval vessels moved out to sea—just far enough to elude shore batteries.

Then it happened again.

As the North counterattacked, several large tremors and a small tidal wave aided their efforts. Neither "natural" action did much damage to buildings—just civilian psyches as people of the South felt the earth move and caught glimpses of the strange screeching objects flying low and fast overhead.

The random explosions.

The counterattack continued as planned. Many soldiers were said to have died on both sides as the small nation sunk into turmoil, and now—mainly due to the renewed lack of verifiable reportage—international indifference.

———————

Even Marion lost interest.

She stopped reading about Phnongtuk—the rare article attempting examinations or explanations of what might be happening—because she found it frustrating, boring, and unsettling all at the same time. Better to lay off or ignore it completely. With few shows on the 24/7 cable-news spectrum showing any interest, she felt free to surf channels with little chance of encountering anything disturbing.

One afternoon while eating lunch, Marion turned to The New Health Channel, where doctors, therapists, and other professionals spoke about depression and recovery, life-changing events—their negative effects as well as positive possibilities for personal growth—generalized coping skills for those facing life's most difficult challenges.

Marion concluded that no one anywhere could dream up a life challenge remotely close to what she had endured, but she ate her sandwich and watched anyway.

What else did she have?

She had stopped taking Carlie's calls to see how she was

doing. Stopped returning them despite her sister's expressed concerns and threats to "come down there and see for myself that you're okay."

Marion sent her a Washington Monument postcard from the Sixties and wrote on the back only, "I'm fine. Tall and proud. Stay home."

But Marion was not fine. She was depressed — deeply, darkly depressed — her television habits reflecting her profoundly troubled state. Her experiences in Phnongtuk hung around her like tuberculosis in a cave.

After a few weeks of avoiding anything to do with the place, she realized how impacted she had been with any of that news — all of it stirring up anxieties so deep she could no longer locate the source.

If any reports came on from anywhere in that part of the world, she could not change the channel quickly enough. Thankfully, since little was being reported anymore, she rarely had to leap for the remote. But she remained vigilant.

Instead, Marion Cooper focused her attention on old familiar movies and sitcoms. The bar buddies on *Cheers* became *her* buddies, and the friends on *Friends,* her friends. Bickering *Housewives* from anywhere were left to parade their histrionics for others. Marion needed happy.

Not that it helped much.

She tried to fit her new routine into her old frame of mind, but everything slowly ground to a halt. She did not so much as go off the rails as feel like they were slowly converging in front of her, slowing her life to a full stop — like snowplowing on skis.

She wore the same robe and pajamas, bunny slippers, day in and day out. She began to dread leaving the house for any reason — even food. Her geranium had long since died, along with Marion's hope for a better world.

Then she discovered that her favorite small, local grocer had begun a delivery service. Hallelujah! She paid with her card over the phone once, then the store kept her information on file so that all she had to do was call with her list and within the hour, her groceries appeared on her backdoor stoop, as she requested for privacy.

"Please have them knock lightly, then leave," she told the order taker every time.

Cecily Mayer gave up knocking to check on her neighbor. Norman determined that Marion was "kooky and out of her mind," which suited Marion fine. She heard them talking about her one day across the fence and smiled.

Now, they would stay away forever.

One early afternoon, after making her usual ham and cheese on rye with the store's own garlic dills on the side and a lunch-size bag of bar-b-cue Lays—fuck the sodium—Marion made her way back to the den and her TV table, flipping on the big screen through a series of no-gos until she came across a woman host she did not recognize.

"I'm Stephanie Golde, and this is *You Win!* The show about...*winning!*"

Before Marion could find the remote—she was sitting on it—Stephanie Golde announced that "today's theme is 'Surviving the loss of a loved one in a natural disaster.'"

Marion stopped digging for the remote.

Apparently, *You Win!* was not so much about winning as enduring.

Stephanie went on to announce that "today's guest is Richard Holliman, who lost his wife of thirty-six years during the cataclysmic events in Southeast Asia that began with an earthquake — an awful tsunami — and ended in war."

Marion held her sandwich, mouth agape, but did not take another bite.

"Richard," Stephanie said, "welcome to the program."

Her guest said, "Thank you for having me," and Marion's mind raced back to Phnongtuk and the quake. Had she seen it happen?

He looked familiar.

In her mind's eye, Marion could see Richard Holliman and his wife standing on a corner one moment and the next being swept away — his wife sucked under the water....

But was it an actual memory or a PTSD-induced false recollection? Though the image *felt* authentic, Marion could not say for sure.

It didn't matter. There he was on television, sitting on a stylish leather couch across from emcee Stephanie Golde — smiling.

Without his wife.

Marion set her sandwich down as Stephanie let her audience know that, "Richard lost his beloved wife Angelee on day three of their forty-third wedding anniversary vacation when they were swept away by — "

Marion dug frantically for the remote and turned off the flat screen — then sat shaking. She could feel her teeth rattling.

Her bones.

But a rush of blood flooded her body and brain, and she had to see.

When the screen came back to life, Richard was saying, "... a fluke, without question. Why was she lost, but I was washed onto the roof of a building that survived? We can never know God's reasons for such choices, only that He makes them — or doesn't."

Stephanie gave a professional response. "To be fair, you were washed near that building, and fought like the dickens to get yourself up on that roof."

"True," Richard said. "Others tried but didn't make it."

"Then you helped several others to safety. More than a dozen, as I recall."

"Something like that," Richard said humbly.

His host said, "Let's remind our viewers of just how crazy that scene was." She turned to the camera and said, "I've been advised to warn our audience that some of the scenes shown in this cellphone footage are disturbing."

Marion braced.

As shaky images recorded by victims of the quake/tsunami came across the screen, showing buildings tipping and collapsing, rivers of debris-clogged ocean water rushing up streets, pushing cars and bodies into alleys that ended abruptly — crushing everyone and everything — Marion's body trembled.

The footage still as fresh as yesterday.

Stephanie's voiceover explained, "In this freezeframe shot by a local woman who survived only to discover that she had lost all three of her young children, we can actually see my guest Richard on that roof, lifting other survivors from the raging waters to safety.

The vid-cap paused, and a light circle highlighted Richard on the roof, lifting an older woman onto the flat roof, the raging water just a foot below.

Marion sat transfixed. She had not seen that moment, but she had seen many like it. Moments that would live in her DNA until she died.

When the image of the two sitting in the studio came back

on, Richard said, "We were lucky that the water only rose another six inches or so and that the building didn't collapse under the shaking and the surge. We were all grievously lucky."

Stephanie asked, "Why do you say 'grievously' lucky?"

"Because," Richard said solemnly, "even in those moments of total chaos and confusion, you realize that though you are safe, it may not last—you may well still die—but more so that others have died, are dying all around you, and will continue to die, probably for days. Weeks."

The small in-studio audience moaned empathically, feeling some of what he felt on that day, likely knowing they could never know the full extent of it—and hoping they never would.

Marion reached for a Kleenex.

Stephanie turned to the camera and said, "When we come back, How Richard came to accept his wife's passing—his own tale of survival." Richard smiled, seemingly at ease, so Marion could not change the channel. She continued to hang on to every word.

At the end of the show, Marion grabbed up her phone and dialed their toll-free number.

When someone answered, Marion said, "Yes, hello, my name is Marion Cooper. I watched your show today, and...you said at the end that if a viewer would like to talk with a guest, you will contact the guest, for the viewer, and...I'd like to talk to Richard Holliman, please. If that's possible."

When the production assistant on the other end explained that it was up to the guest if contact would be made, Marion said, "Of course." She provided a CliffsNotes version of her Phnongtuk story and left her phone number and email.

She then hung up and mentally wrung her hands for twenty minutes, pacing the entire house several times, wondering

if she had done the right thing.
　　　Or the worst thing.

25

A torrential downpour beat down on the concrete roof above the rebar grid over the two cells where Dan and Lana had been moved, from which they were able to watch the other be roughly interrogated. At least they were dry and allowed clothing.

They were still being given nutrition—some indefinable goop to be washed down by rainwater. Dan remained amazed that neither had contracted dysentery, but for some reason, their food, water, and *accommodations* seemed relatively sterile.

Two metal planks had been attached to either side of the bars separating the two cells. At mealtime, several masked guards came into each cell and physically dragged both Lana and Dan into a corner to wait as other guards placed bowls of gruel and cups of rainwater on each plank table. Then the guards backed out.

Dan always rushed to the meal, followed reluctantly by Lana. This time, she did not join him to sup.

"You need to eat," he told her, wolfing down his slop.

"There are bugs in it," she said.

"Protein," Dan said. "And hey, if it was good enough for

Anthony Bourdain, it's good enough for me."

"Ick," Lana said, lackluster.

Dan had noticed Lana looking gaunt. "Are you feeling okay?"

"No," she said.

"Depressed?"

"What do you think?"

Dan stood, reaching his hand through the bars. "We have to beat this," he said. "They want to keep us alive. That's why they're feeding us this crap."

"So they can kill us later," Lana said, oscillating between defeat and anger.

"I don't think so," Dan said, scraping his finger around the bowl and licking it clean. "They believe we know something they want or need to know. Or maybe we're just being kept as potential bargaining chips. Who knows? But as long as they keep thinking that, whatever it is, I'd say we're good to go."

"You don't know that."

"We're here, aren't we?"

Lana raised her face.

"Right?" he asked her. "You understand this, I know. If they wanted us dead...."

"We'd be dead," she said.

"So," he said. "Come. Eat." He waited for her to stand. "It's awful, I'll grant you that, whatever it is—"

"Krung Lah," Lana said.

"What's that?" Dan said.

"Local delicacy."

"Ah, there's the spirit I was looking for!"

He sounded as happy as a high school math teacher who had just lifted a failing student out of a self-imposed low-grades ditch of doom and inspired her to pursue a career in physics.

When Lana got to the bars, she reached out and took his hand. "You're a good man, Daniel Cooper."

A guard screamed—unintelligible words that translated as "NO TOUCHING!"

Lana retrieved her hand and sat down to eat.

Dan said, "No one's called me Daniel in…thirty years. Except general Battery Cables."

Lana said, "Not even Marion?"

"Especially Marion," he said. "She was sort of raped by a cousin named Daniel when she was twelve or so."

"Sort of?" Lana said. "How do you 'sort of' rape someone?"

"He was so soft he couldn't get it in. Though, as she said—some sort of defense thing—she 'had to give him credit for trying.'"

"That's…disturbing," Lana said.

"Marion is a complex individual," Dan said. His words held respect, if not hope.

Lana looked up from her bowl. "Gruel's pretty good today."

"Not bad for King Kong," he said.

"Krung Lah."

"Meh."

They managed a laugh—then, just as quickly, Lana started to jerk.

Tears followed.

"Hey," Dan said, reaching back through the bars to take her hand. "What?"

Another untranslated, "NO TOUCHING!"

Dan retreated—and glared.

Through her tears, Lana said, "I'm so sorry I got you into

this."

Dan said, "None of us are perfect."

"That's for damn sure," Lana said, wiping her final tear, bucking up.

Dan got quiet. Sat back. "Do you know what we were arguing about that day? Marion and I? Did you hear any of it?"

"Not enough to know what it was."

"I found a lonely young divorcee the night before and snuck out to screw her."

Lana looked up, surprised. "You?"

"Pretty sad, huh?" he said. "On vacation with my wife of two decades, and I go off half-cocked to bang some Lonely Hearts club poster girl on her post-divorce getaway-and-get-even trip."

"Sounds like you were more than half-cocked," Lana said. Then, "Aw, she was looking for it. That's why she was there. And you'd been faithful for two decades. You were probably easier to haul in than a sixteen-year-old in a strip club."

"Doesn't make it right," Dan said. "And who said I was faithful all those years?"

"I didn't say it did, and I didn't say you were," Lana said. "But it does make you human. Like you said, we all make mistakes. We aren't perfect. We fuck up." She gave a slight grunt. "Was she at least hot?"

"Not as hot as you in that little bikini that day," Dan said, grinning.

"Oh, you are bad," Lana said with a dark chuckle.

And…was she *blushing*?

"Truth hurts," he said.

"Fuck off," she said. "But I can see why Marion was less than interested in my friendliness."

"Hey," he said. "You saved us."

"And brought you here."

"No one's perfect," he said again. "Finish your Krom Dum."

"Krung Lah," she corrected.

"I know."

"It's a root."

"Yeah, I know that, too."

Before Lana could respond, a loud clang came—making her jump. "Jesus," she said. "What now?"

"Be strong, babe."

As the locks were being thrown and the cage door opened, Lana looked at Dan. "Babe?"

"Sorry," he said—surprised, himself. "Slipped out."

"Well, well, well," the awful, familiar voice said. "My most favorite American prisoners. How long has it been?"

Dan said, "Long enough to be sick of hearing you talk."

"I meant," the general said—seemingly unbothered by the dig—"since I gave you a surprise."

Lana repeated, "Oh, Jesus." Her skin, body, and orifices braced for impact.

"Did you find the Krung Lah to your liking, today?"

"Yeah," Dan said. "Really enjoyed the extra bugs."

"Happy to provide the nourishment," the general said. "And you are right. If I had wanted you dead, you would be dead."

Both prisoners looked at him with hatred even though they knew they were being eavesdropped on constantly.

"Come," he said, waving for them to follow.

Knowing it could not be that easy, they remained seated.

"Come, come!" he repeated. "Today, I have a special treat for you!"

"Oh, Jesus," Lana said a third time.

Dan said, "You can't beat us in here?"

"No, no, no!" the masked man said. "Nothing of the kind. Come. Come! You will like this one. I promise!"

When they still did not move, he nodded for his masked guards to help.

Lana and Dan stood.

"Good, good! Much better! Much better!" their tormenter said.

Lana said, "You're repeating yourself a lot today. Did you forget your Alzheimer's medicine?"

"Very good, very good," he said. "Oh!" he then said, feigning delight. "And look. I did it again!"

He left the cell, chortling.

The unamused guards waited. Dan and Lana walked from their individual cells out into the hallway to be led around the corner.

Lana said, "This place is bigger than I thought."

Dan said, "Always a surprise around here."

They remained tense, unsure of what might await them — what new pain, degradation, or cruelty.

The guards stopped them at a different cell — larger, with the same cement roof over video cameras and the rebar grid, and one difference, a mattress on the floor. No sheets, but wide enough for two, and it even looked clean.

A table had been set with two plates of what appeared to be actual food, a lit candle, and a caldron-sized bottle of red liquid.

"What is this, our last meal?" Dan asked.

"Cyanide or polonium?" Lana said.

"Neither," their captor said, happily. "Red wine. Though I

cannot vouch for its provenance. As I have mentioned, alcohol is not allowed in our country."

"So, where'd you get it?" Lana asked.

"Imported," was all he said with a coarse chuckle. Then he turned away, "Enjoy."

And he left!

Dan called out, "What's with the fucking candle?"

The guards left.

Lana strolled over to the table, looked it over, and said, "He's trying to romance us."

"Good luck with that," Dan said.

"Hey!" Lana said. "At least give me some respect here. You said I looked hot."

"That was before you stopped eating."

Lana looked down at her thinning frame and said, "Then let's fix that."

She moved to the table. Dan followed. They sat opposite each other and stared at the food. It looked decent and smelled fabulous. But then, anything was better than gruel.

Dan sniffed the wine. "Smells like wine. A little Annie Greensprings-ish, but whatever."

"I could use a good buzz," Lana said and poured herself a cup — then Dan.

"You think it's poisoned?" he said.

"You know what, dear?" Lana said. "At this point, I don't care."

She downed it in one slug.

Then she refilled and raised her cup as if to toast.

Dan said, "I think I'll wait a minute to see if you keel over."

"Fair enough," Lana said and drank the second cup. Then she said, "You're gonna have to catch up," as she poured herself a third.

"Maybe we should keep some around for later," Dan said — still stalling.

Watching her closely.

"They don't want that," Lana said. "They want us to eat a decent meal, get drunk, and fuck each other like freshmen in their first mixed dorm."

Dan reluctantly said, "Get us to care about each other."

She said, "Oh, don't worry about that. I gave up caring about men I fuck a long time ago."

That made Dan laugh out loud — and gave him the courage to drink his wine down in one gulp. He had to admit, "Not bad." Then he amended, "Not good, but considering...."

"Not bad at all," she said.

And they toasted and drank and ate.

And fucked.

26

Marion vacuumed the house, washed linens, weeded her new roses, and even cleaned the garage, giving another few loads to Goodwill—anything that no longer had a use.

Dan's golf clubs and his kayak.

She kept his tools in case she might want to take on a project at some point.

Every day, she turned on Stephanie Golde's show to check out the survival topic for the day. Mostly the shows had to do with diseases—how to survive one, latest developments in treatment, how to survive a loved one's life-threatening malady.

So, mostly Marion switched off the set and went back to cleaning or organizing or cooking or backyard gardening.

Never the front.

She even tried crocheting. When her pink hat with ears did not turn out so well, she put her needles and yarn in a drawer and never opened it again.

Each night, she read before bed—mostly magazines and benign literary fiction. She briefly attempted a few thrillers, but as soon as the story got thrilling, her heart rate increased close to the level of palpitations, and she went back to *Ladies Home Journal*.

Marion had never been a *Ladies Home Journal* type. But it was safe.

Most nights, she read until her eyes felt heavy, then she put her reading material on the nightstand and closed her eyes. When they popped back open, she turned on the light and read some more.

"Rinse and repeat," she heard herself say more than once.

Then she got the phone call from Richard Holliman, the tsunami survivor from *You Win!* He was in D.C. on business and agreeable to meeting for a late lunch.

––––––––––

The popular restaurant had been packed as usual, but by the time Marion arrived, on time, to find Richard waiting on a bench by the greeter's podium, several tables had become available.

No waiting.

The conversation proved difficult, awkward, stilted — everything that Marion had imagined it would be.

And a little more.

Richard spoke of his great love for his deceased wife, Angelee. They had met in college, Dartmouth, and were the first interracial couple in their group — maybe in the entire university. Her parents had both been medical researchers for the CDC, his engineers for the Department of Transportation, so they hit it off right away in an elective anatomy class. She went on to be a pediatrician; he designed complicated commercial stairwells and fancy foyers for wealthy New Yorkers.

They had three children, all of whom did well in school and went on to professional careers. He had taken up sailing, something he and Angelee had talked about doing but never got around to trying. Now, he found the water, wind, and relative silence comforting and expansive.

Marion seemed surprised that little to none of this information was mentioned on Golde's show.

"Stephanie is more interested in the emotions of loss and the struggle for understanding—'reformation,' as I call it," Richard said. To clarify, he stated, in engineering terms, "I had to re-form my life, as it had been entirely built around our life together."

He paused briefly, then said, "The kids helped."

"I'm sure they did," Marion said, thinking that had she and Dan ever had children, they might be of comfort to her in her time of need.

On the other hand, she thought, *my luck, they'd probably all be drug addicts or Republicans.*

"You're smiling," Richard said—as a question. Marion demurred and said little more for the rest of the meal.

But at one point, over gelato, the impact of the meeting caught up with her, and several tears ran down Marion's cheeks.

Richard took her hand and squeezed gently. Respectfully. Fully understanding. Marion nodded thanks and retrieved her hand to daub at her cheeks.

That being their only contact.

At the door on leaving, Richard thanked Marion for lunch—she had insisted on paying since she invited him, and he was a guest in D.C.—and they said goodbye. No hugs were offered, and no other plans were made to speak again.

That night in bed, Marion felt something in her gut and set her book down in her lap. She removed her glasses and put them on her nightstand. Then she let go a single, deep, wrenching sob. Just one.

Then she was done.

The next morning, Marion Cooper arose from the first night of deep sleep she had enjoyed since returning to the States, going on two years earlier. The sun was out, the air crisp and dry, the world settled but vivid.

After enjoying — truly enjoying — her coffee on the back porch by her dead geranium, she dead-headed columbine buds, trimmed her roses, and threw the geranium away in her compost bin.

Life was changing for Alanda as well. Ashton was sharing her bed.

He was a good, if somewhat inexperienced lover, but Alanda was patient. She had already trained one young man; the second was much easier.

Working on his body and his approach to lovemaking was one thing; giving him confidence was another.

Mornings for Alanda had become easier as time passed but more difficult for Ashton. He felt tremendous guilt and said so.

Repeatedly.

Finally, one morning after an energetic session, Alanda decided to confront their problem. "Ashton," she said simply. "It's okay."

He rolled away and said, "No. It isn't. It's not okay. You're married. You're a married woman. I...I don't do that. Not with married women."

Alanda rolled closer, wrapped her ankle over his knee, ran her hand across his bare chest softly, playfully, and told him, "It's a new world. For both of us. And it's time for both of us to move on."

"But it's wrong," he said.

"No," she said. "It's right. It's very right."

He looked at her with watery, fearful eyes.

She said, "What happened was terrible, but it's past. It's gone like the dinosaurs."

She got a chuckle from him. But he said, "That seems kind of cold."

"It's reality, Ashton," Alanda said, plainly. "You said yourself he wasn't coming home. It's been almost two years, and he hasn't come home. He's not coming home. I understand that, now."

She bit her lip.

"It hasn't been easy to accept that, but you've helped," she said. "And I don't mean just the sex, which is wonderful. But the companionship. The acceptance. The…tolerance for my pain. And the respect."

"I just…." Ashton said. "I don't want to be 'that guy.'"

"You're not," Alanda said. "You're my rock. You've been my anchor."

Ashton lifted up enough to look his new lover in the eyes and said, "And you are my flower. My garden. My perfect blossom. My everything."

Alanda lay still. Then she put her head back down and said, "Tell me more," with a smile.

Ashton was happy to do just that. He said, "Alanda, I never knew I could love someone the way I love you. I had no idea it could be like this. *Feel* like this. So…total and…full. But I would rather leave this minute than stay and cause you any hurt or trouble, any pain in any way. I swear, I'd rather die in a ditch somewhere like a dog than cause you any pain. Hell, I'd go back over *there* rather than hurt you or make any trouble for you. If I had any hint that any bad would come of this, I would leave this instant and never come back."

Alanda smiled softly and said, "Stay."

Ashton smiled. Finally. And he said, "What about your parents?"

They had continued to keep their distance.

Alanda said, "They'll come around." Then she added, "At least you're not White."

Ashton chuckled with her, and they clutched each other tightly. It felt good, and it felt right, and it felt like it would never end.

27

In the darkest jungle, bugs and the occasional snake made their way into the cells, depending on the season. Dan and Lana stopped noticing.

They had been "shacking up together," as she joked, for three months—months without torture. The good food did not last—no more wine—but they had been left alone, seemingly forgotten.

Lana put back some of the weight she lost, and the two exercised regularly to stay as fit as possible—mentally and physically. But her eyes were often dull, and her skin tone occasionally sallow. Still, she did her best to hang in, and Dan never let up on the encouragement.

Then, one peaceful afternoon, birds chirping in the trees outside, as Dan and Lana groomed each other like baboons—Lana's take on it as they picked bugs from each other's hair—they heard fast footsteps.

"Crap," Dan said, and Lana agreed.

"I was hoping they were done with us," Lana said.

Moments later, guards unlocked the door and shoved a

golden-locked surfer dude into their cell.

"Lucas?" Dan said, not believing what he was seeing as the guards re-locked the grate and left without a word.

Lucas was well-groomed, shaved, and wearing newish local-styled clothes. Even shoes. "Hey," he said. "I thought you guys were dead. That's what they told me."

"That's what they told us about you," Dan said.

"Well, I'm not. And you aren't. And here we are." He sounded positively cheery.

That would not hold.

Their masked interrogator appeared a moment later, his usual pompous demeanor worn like an insignia — a rack of them.

He said, "Lucas Aaron Tucker, who went to his CIA recruiter at Stanford but was told he was too stupid to be an agent." The general shook his head. "You may do with him as you please. We have no further use for him."

And he left.

The three prisoners stared at each other. Lana and Dan shared a stern look that communicated a singular thought. *They are using him to get us to loosen up and talk.*

Lucas said, "Is this where you've been all along?"

Lana said, "They move us around."

"Oh," he said. "They had me in the Little House. That's what they call it."

"Where is it?" Dan asked, thinking that Lucas seemed to be putting on an air of diffidence.

"About ten minutes away, in the jungle," Lucas said. "Walking."

Dan asked, "Did you see anything outside here?"

"A few guards," Lucas said, shrugging. "I forget their names. They were new." His eyes darted from one side of the cell to the other.

Dan asked what kind of weapons they had.

Lucas shrugged again, seemingly irritated, and said, "How would I know? I mean, they let me shoot them every now and then, but I don't know what they are. Automatic rifles, I guess. Handguns. Pistols and shit." Another shrug. "Machine guns, maybe."

Dan thinking, *No wonder the CIA didn't want him.*

Lana scratched at a persistent bug bite. "So, you've been, what? Just...*hanging out*? One of the *dudes*."

Lucas said, "Sort of. I mean, I was a prisoner, like you, only I was in a house with a bed, in a room, with a guard outside, and bars on the windows."

Dan only then noticed that Lucas was shaking. His eyes still darting like a cornered animal looking for an escape.

Lana noticed as well. "Lucas? Are you okay?"

He gave a weak, if angry, "No."

"What happened?" Dan asked. "What did they do to you?"

"They made me...do things," Lucas said, quietly. Tears starting to roll down his face.

Lana said, "They did that to us, too."

"It hurt," Lucas said.

"Yes," Lana said, and went over to touch his arm gently.

"They called me a faggot," he said. "I'm not."

"No," Lana said. "Of course not."

"They did it almost every day," Lucas said, coming unglued — as if none of his calm before had existed. "Sometimes all day," he said. "This...big...ugly guy with...."

"We know," Dan said. "He came here, too."

Lucas burst into full-blown sobbing.

Dan and Lana sighed as one, feeling worse for young Lucas than themselves.

But suddenly, Lucas lunged at Dan and screamed, "Why didn't you tell them what they wanted to know! Why didn't you tell them! They kept doing things to me because you wouldn't tell them! They told me. You…you fuckers!"

He glared back and forth between Dan and Lana.

She said, calmly, "That wasn't why they did it, Lucas. That's just what they said to make you hate us. So you'd come back here and get us to say those things they want to hear."

"Then why don't you tell them!"

He screamed and cried, red and terrified, angry and confused.

"Because we don't know what they want to hear," Dan said, as soothingly as possible. "They won't tell us."

"Then make something up!" Lucas yelled.

Lana said, "We tried that. Didn't work."

"Well, then just…do *something*!" Lucas yelled. "Make them stop!"

Dan said, even if he did not wholly believe it, "I think it's over for you, Lucas. You're safe here. With us."

Lucas looked up, wanting to believe. "You think so?"

"I hope so," Dan said, honestly. He looked to Lana for help.

She said, "Lucas," and he looked at her, pleading with his eyes. "If they had wanted you dead," she said, "they would have killed you."

"I wish they had!" he cried.

"No," Lana said, steadily. "It's always better to be alive."

"Not when they're fucking you in the ass for fucking ever!"

Lana tried a new approach—from experience. "But you

survived. You made it," she said. "That's your mind being strong. That's *you* being strong, Lucas. You survived it. You're alive. You need to be happy about that. Okay?"

Lucas let that float around in his head for a few moments, then said, "What about you guys?"

Dan said, "They rough us up pretty bad from time to time, trying to get us to tell them whatever it is they think we know or whatever. They'll probably make you watch it."

"I don't *want* to watch it. I don't want to ever see anything like any of this shit ever again," he said.

"That may not be possible," Dan said, again opting for truth. "But, like Lana said, you made it this far. That took courage and strength. No matter what you think of yourself. No matter how much you think you let yourself down. You didn't. You did what you had to do to survive. They gave you no options, Lucas. None. Right?"

"No," Lucas agreed.

"So now," Dan said, "we make the best of whatever else comes, okay? Whatever else they throw at us, we stay strong together. Can you do that?"

"I don't know," Lucas said.

Lana encouraged him. "I think you can. You've been braver than you think."

"I'm alive," he said, looking for further encouragement.

"Exactly," she said.

They stood in silence for several moments, then Lucas stepped over to Dan and threw his arms around him, crying. "It was so terrible," he said, sobbing. "I thought they were going to kill me every day." And his worst memory, "Sometimes I wished they would."

"That's normal," Dan said and patted him on the back.

"But they didn't. And you made it."

"I made it," Lucas said, as if beginning to accept the notion—that it might not be out of reach. Then he pulled away, sheepish, and sat in one of the two crude chairs, wiping at his nose and sniffling.

When he nodded to himself—as if acknowledging his survival—Lana took the other chair across from him to ask, "Did they tell you what happened, Lucas? What *is* happening? Out there, in the country."

"Oh yeah," Lucas said, matter-of-factly. "They told me everything. Showed me pictures. Played videos. Told me everything about everything, I guess. Like I was some kind of fucking *pet* or something." His bitterness coming back through.

"Like what?" Dan asked. "What did they show you?"

"The UFOs, the attacks," Lucas said.

"UFOs?" Lana said, glancing at Dan.

"Yeah," Lucas said offhandedly. "They have them in a warehouse somewhere. By that big laser gun thing."

Lana and Dan—having been completely out of that news loop—shared looks of concern tempered with disbelief.

"We don't know anything about any of that, Lucas," Dan said. "They haven't told us or shown us anything."

"It's all real," Lucas said. "The whole world knows it, now."

"Knows what?" Lana asked.

"About the space aliens helping them win the war."

Lana said, "Space aliens?" and Dan said, "The war is over?"

"Not yet," Lucas said. "But they've won. The South just won't recognize it."

Dan recognized the sounds of propaganda believed. He

said, "And they're winning with...aliens and UFOs?"

"Yeah," Lucas said, as if he could not believe they would question it or him.

"And how do you know this?" Lana said.

"The pictures," Lucas said. "Videos." He shrugged as if they were incontrovertible evidence.

"Of aliens and UFOs?" Dan said.

"No," Lucas said. "Not the aliens. They don't want to be photographed. Just their spaceships and shit. The Big Beam Machine."

Lana and Dan both felt as if they had been transported into a parallel universe—or a B-movie. She said, "Can you describe the UFOs to us?"

"Sure," he said. "They look like...well, how you think they'd look. Round. Metal. Weird." He thought back. "I think some of them are more, what do you call it? Cigar-shaped. You know, long and thin, kind of. But maybe with round wings or something." He shrugged. "They were in the videos, flying past. You know, like, overhead and all. Dropping bombs or shooting beams or something. And they sound scary as hell."

"And you saw this? Heard this?" Dan said. "Videos of this."

"Uh-huh," Lucas said. "They had bunches. They're all over the news. From people's cellphones, down in the South. They're all liars," he said.

"Who is, Lucas?"

"The South people. They say they're being killed and shit for no reason. But they started it because they don't want reunification. But reunification is best for everyone. You know, for the whole country. But they don't want it. They want war. So the aliens came down to help the North and stop the South so that everyone can live in harmony."

Dan's wide-eyed *Wow!* look was echoed by Lana. Neither saw any use in pointing out that men from the North had been raping Lucas for two years.

Dan said, "Did they show you anything else?"

"Oh yeah," Lucas said, almost proudly. "All kinds of shit. They even brought a piece of one of the UFOs for me to hold. It weighed, like, nothing. It was amazing. As big as that table, and it weighed, like, an ounce or something. Almost like it wasn't there. And they showed me videos of them beating it with hammers and big machines and shooting laser beams at it, and nothing happened. They can't be destroyed."

"What else?" Dan asked, patiently.

"Um, they had videos of the Big Beam Machine and when it blew up Sur Nam and those towns and shit. I mean, like, poof, and they were gone."

"What towns and...Sur Nam?" Lana said.

"It's a mountain," Lucas said, almost disinterested. "It was all over the news. They did a demonstration. Then they blew up some towns in the south. Where the main resistance was. Just one shot, and boom, they were gone. It was kind of awesome, really. Like a sci-fi movie."

"It sounds like it," Lana said, flashing a glance at Dan.

"And computers," Lucas remembered. "Supercomputers. Towers of them in secret warehouses where they said they could monitor every movement anywhere for hundreds of miles. They can detect a cat landing on the ground from a hundred miles away."

"What does that have to do with aliens?" Dan said.

"The aliens taught them how to build them—the computers," he said. Then laughed. "It's funny because they said someday they'd use the computers to get rid of the aliens. They said the aliens are really stupid and trusting, and they'll never leave earth alive."

Lana said, "They say that to us almost every day—and here we are."

"Yeah, well, we're humans," Lucas said. "We're smart." He looked at Lana. "And strong."

Lana smiled benevolently. "Right. Good," she said—and looked to Dan.

Dan read her plea for help. "Do you want something to eat, Lucas? We haven't started into this yet." He offered a bowl of gruel.

Lucas turned up his nose. "No, I'm good. I had ribs last night. What *is* that?"

"It's what they give us to keep us alive," Lana said.

Lucas turned away. "I know you don't believe me—no one does." He seemed to be including himself with his captors.

Dan and Lana seeing Stockholm Syndrome all over the kid's face.

"It's true, though," Lucas said of the photos, videos, and stories. "I saw it all."

Dan nodded at him and said, "Well, thank you for telling us what you saw."

"Yeah, thanks," Lana said. "That explains a lot."

"Cool," Lucas said. "It was pretty weird when they first told me, but the more I saw, it blew my mind, man. It's crazy out there."

Dan and Lana silently agreed.

"I'm tired now," Lucas said. "I need to sleep some." He walked for the mattress on the floor.

"Go ahead," Lana said. "You need to rest."

"Yeah, I do," Lucas said as he laid down. "I miss Alanda," he said. "I'm not gay."

28

As Alanda and Ashton spent more quality time together and their love grew, over in D.C., Marion had moved on to her new life as well—alone.

She allowed the grey in her hair free reign and *traded in* for a shorter 'do. Two older lesbians hit on her in one day, but she passed politely. "It's just a haircut," she told them. "Purely a maintenance issue. Not a statement."

They thanked her and moved on.

On checking her bank account—Dan's name was still on it as well—Marion realized she had not been paying much attention to finances as everything had always been on autopay. She knew that she was safe financially—Dan's death benefits had kicked in—but she did not realize just how safe.

Each monthly check put more into "their" account than Dan and she had earned together at any time during their lives together. In short, Marion Cooper was flush.

The redecorating began.

Always careful with a dollar, Marion searched catalogs for bargains on the eclectic mix of furnishings and art she had always wanted but never felt comfortable buying. She brought in painters and an interior decorator — whom she quickly fired for being ridiculous — and even took to rolling her own walls.

She hung modern art, replaced her aging bathroom fixtures with new — including a new "shower room" with multiple heads, and redesigned the kitchen on her own.

The Mayers recommended a reliable contractor, who turned out to be a great guy, easygoing, fit and funny. Several post-demo and cabinet re-install beers later, they ended up on the counter, pants around their ankles.

Though he was not married, the man, Ben Quaily, felt bad. "Guilty," he told her, "seeing as how you're married."

Marion said something about it being "on paper" only, though she had never received official notice of Dan's death nor posted one.

"I've never slept with a married woman before," Quaily told her. "It's just not *me*. I never felt right about that."

"It's okay, Ben," Marion assured him. "We didn't sleep."

Though he laughed, Ben told her he could not repeat their lust again — which was fine with Marion. Once had been enough. Uncontrollable lust had reared its lovely head — like that one time before, several years earlier, the one she almost confessed to on the beach in Phnongtuk that day.

She had hoped that by telling Dan about her fling — alcohol was involved — that he would be honest about his indiscretions, and they could begin to have a healing conversation.

Then an earthquake and tsunami happened.

With Ben Quaily, lust had been instant — and just as instantly satisfied. Marion had wondered; her wonder was quenched, and now she could do without.

Until the mood struck again — if it ever would. Marion had

her doubts.

The kitchen turned out better than she had hoped, for less than she had planned to spend, and Ben went on to his next project. Marion wondered if he had been honest or was already boffing another married woman on her new countertops.

Marion Cooper didn't care; she was free—free from her past, free from her future, free from her marriage.

Dan was dead.

Marion could not fully concede that point, but she had come to accept it. After all, some twenty-seven months had passed with no word, no return, no sign. For all practical intents and purposes, she told herself, *I'm a widow*.

Marion had no desire to find a replacement, no desire to file for divorce, no inclination to retake her maiden name—no desire to change anything at all about her newfound freedom and lifestyle, figuring that this was as happy as a person could ever hope to be in this life. Asking lawyers to get involved in sorting out the will and their possessions felt like begging trouble—not to mention the expense.

No, it was better to do nothing. That's what Marion decided. Just ride the happy train until she was forced off the rails—or Dan returned.

That possibility seeming as remote as walking to the Moon.

There was sadness—memories, good and bad—because there *was* a past. But there was the present, now. And the present was good. And Marion felt whole.

And that felt right.

———

In Chicago, Alanda did opt for divorce, certain that Lucas was never coming home. Despite Ashton's reluctance, Alanda filed the requisite Order of Notice by Publication, then the divorce petition.

But first, she called Marion.

"Hi, it's Alanda," she said. "From Phnongtuk."

"I remember," Marion said, sipping a gin and tonic on her new back patio, out of sight of the world, a new James Patterson on her side table.

Thrillers had become fun.

"How are you doing?" she asked.

"Good," Alanda told her.

But something seemed missing in her tone. So Marion asked, "Why did you call now, Alanda? Did you hear something? About Lucas?"

"No," Alanda said, "nothing. That's why I'm calling."

"Are you wanting to know if I've heard anything?" Marion said.

"Not really," Alanda said. "I was just wondering...how you're doing."

Over the years, being married to a man who did not openly share his thoughts or feelings, Marion had become adept at reading people. "Are you asking me if I have accepted Dan's death? That he is never coming back to me?"

Alanda paused. "I guess so," she said.

Marion took a sip of her delightful cocktail, set it down, and sat upright. "Alanda, do you want me to give you some advice?"

"I don't know," Alanda said.

"Let me put it another way," Marion said. "Are you looking for permission?"

Alanda did not respond.

Marion tried to imagine what Alanda looked like these

days. Where she was. What she was doing. If she had found someone new. So she asked.

Alanda told her.

"Really?" Marion said, genuinely surprised. "He found you in Chicago?"

"Yes," Alanda said. "It's quite remarkable, isn't it?"

"I don't know if I would use that word," Marion said honestly. "It was apparent that he was enamored of you…back there."

"Was it that obvious?" Alanda said.

Marion laughed. "Are you asking if it was obvious that you were as interested in him as he was in you? If you are, the answer is maybe. You were under a lot of stress, as we all were. But yes, to some degree, I thought I detected some interest in there — mixed with the terror of the situation."

Alanda stayed quiet for a moment. Then she said, "We're thinking of getting married."

Ahh. There it was.

"Well," Marion said, "in that case, I don't think I'm the right person to be asking for permission."

Alanda objected. "I didn't mean permission to marry him."

"I know, dear," Marion said. "But I'm trying to make the point that it's your life. Now. Then. The future. It's yours to decide."

"I know that, I guess," Alanda said, echoing vague uncertainty.

"But I will say this," Marion told her. "There comes a time in life, and these are difficult times when they show their ugly heads, that we have to make difficult decisions. We can't be slaves to our pasts, even if those past times were good — even wonderful.

As they say, all good things come to an end. I'm not sure I believe that necessarily. But I do believe that whatever our lives were — yours and mine and hundreds of thousands of other poor souls who were unfortunate enough to experience what we did — all of us were changed by those experiences. Changed deeply. More deeply than we will likely ever understand, no matter how long we live. So, to that end, knowing these realities, facing them, and not being afraid of them, we come to a point where we must make a choice, Do we live in those wonderful pasts? Do we remain in those terrible moments, afraid to let go in case something even worse comes to be? Or do we take a chance — and it *is* a chance — do we take a chance and say, 'I will not be held down. I will not be held back. I will not stay in this one place forever. I will go on. I will be afraid. I will be unsure. I will not know how it is going to turn out. But I will take that chance. I will go, and I will see. And if it is not good, if it is bad, I will stop and think and be honest and start over again as many times as it takes. But I will not, I will never, be beaten by memories. I will not.'"

Quite a speech, and even Marion had no idea where it had all come from — other than her own deep insecurities and doubts. Some venting that had needed to occur for a long while, justification for her own difficult choices. Alanda just happened to be the recipient as well as the catalyst.

So, Marion thanked her.

"For what?" Alanda said.

"Letting me get that off my chest," Marion said.

Another quiet spell sat on the other end of the line. Then Alanda said, "Well, I'm glad I could help."

And she hung up.

Marion looked at her phone, perplexed — perhaps piqued — and shrugged.

Then she went back to her gin and tonic and her James Patterson and never gave her situation, or Alanda's, or Alanda, another thought.

29

As the weeks passed, Lucas realized how lucky he had been.

Though he was slow to admit it, what he endured in the Little House may have been worth the trade-off. He'd had a warm shower and shave every day, three square meals, a shared but clean bathroom, and several changes of fresh clothes available.

Now his clothes were filthy, his beard scruffy, his stomach in pain. He had never had to shit in a bucket, much less ten or more times a day when the gruel did not agree with his system. He itched constantly.

Bug bites under his testicles.

But all of that was nothing compared to the intermittent, unpredictable flashes of light, blaring music, and unexpected visits from the general and his entourage, which had become more frequent and threatening.

Something had changed—some deadline was approaching. A need to wrap things up in the jungle prison. Dan and Lana sensed it, whispered about it, and knew it was coming but did not dare mention anything to poor Lucas.

For as quickly as Lana seemed to be declining—she had

lost the weight again and rarely had any color other than ochre in her almost transparent skin — Lucas was worse.

His mental state had careered from mostly acceptant to relentlessly terrified, wholly unsettled, and clearly on the verge of trying or saying anything to make the torture end — not to mention endlessly guilty and ashamed.

He had begun screaming each time the kliegs came on unexpectedly in the night, accompanied by the pounding, high-pitched whining of bad Asian metal rock.

Who knew they even had it?

"STOP IT! STOP IT! JESUS! STOP IT!"

Efforts by Lucas's cellmates to calm him — including cuddling him to sleep on the narrow mattress — became less effective as each unsettling day passed, with every disturbing, intrusive, wearisome, emotionally disruptive attack.

"WHY WON'T THEY STOP? WE DON'T KNOW ANYTHING! MAKE THEM STOP! PLEASE! MAKE THEM STOP!"

Lucas had been reduced to a quivering, tortured shell of the once-fearless Southern California daredevil, unafraid to surf the biggest, gnarliest winter swells, skateboard through sewers at night, and helicopter ski powder in Utah on his rich, White parents' dime.

To date a black woman in college, marry her and move to Chicago.

Lucas Tucker once outraced an avalanche, skiing for all he was worth, faster than he had ever skied, with greater control and precision than he knew he had, narrowly escaping millions of tons of white death.

Laughing giddily the whole way.

And now, here he was, crying like a baby, wetting himself

on a regular basis, disoriented, having lost any understanding of humanity — the complete absence of it in this awful place. Having to be dressed and cleaned by Dan and Lana when they would discover him wandering the cell naked, diarrhea streaming down his legs from his latest bout, screaming epithets at God and his parents for letting this happen.

"WHY DO THEY KEEP DOING THAT! WHY WON'T THEY STOP!

Running to the bars to scream into the lights.

"TURN IT OFF! TURN IT OFF! TURN IT OFF!"

Falling into a heap of weeping, pitiable nothingness.

Dan and Lana considered letting him go, letting him slip away into madness. Death might be easier on the poor kid. But they could not bring themselves to it. Every night, they would retrieve him, lift him up, clean and clothe him, lay him down between them, and hold him until he could fall asleep — even if they could not.

Then the general upped the stakes.

Lights clacked on, music blared, cell locks rattled, the cage door squeaked, and the general entered with his masked, armed men at three one morning.

Tonight would be different. They could all feel it — everyone in the room.

When the kliegs were killed along with the music and normal lights came on, Dan said, "Here we go," under his breath.

Lana did not disagree. "What do you want now, you sick fuck?" was how she put it. "What happened?"

The general smiled under his mask, his dark eyes dancing with prospects. "I knew you would know," he said.

Dan said, "Time is running out."

"For you, perhaps," the general said.

"Are you going to say 'No more games' again?" Dan said. "Or is it again-again."

"Again-again-again," Lana mocked—if weakly.

"We will see who then is laughing," the general said in uncharacteristic, muddled grammar.

Not a good sign.

He asked Lana, "How are you feeling, dear? You appear... pale."

"I'm fine," Lana said.

But Dan had noticed, too—her pallor, lack of energy, and what he guessed was plain mental fatigue. *Who wouldn't show those signs after more than two years in this soul-crushing hellhole?* On rare occasions, even Dan felt like packing it in.

But he said to the general, "She's fine. We're all just dandy. Thank you for your concern."

The general gave a mock smile at his prisoner's sarcasm, then shouted orders to his guards, who snapped-to and went directly to Lucas, who had pulled himself into the far corner as tightly as he could, to disappear into the cement work to become as small and insignificant as possible.

It did not work.

Three soldiers—Lucas recognized their build and movements from seeing them before. He knew their names, too— and used them, imploring them not to hurt him, not to follow orders, to, "Leave me alone, please. You know me! Please!"

To no avail.

They dragged him into the middle of the room and forced him down onto his knees. When he spoke their names again, they beat him. When he begged them to stop in their own language— which they had taught him—they beat him until he stopped.

But this was not his torture for the night.

Lana beseeched the general, "He's a kid. He doesn't know anything. Haven't you brutalized him enough?"

The general stepped over to one of his men to borrow a 9mm sidearm—a Russian GSh-18. He put the muzzle to Lucas's temple and asked Dan and Lana, without introduction, "Who will save Lucas's life tonight?"

Lucas lost his bladder and shouted, "No! Dan! Do something!"

When neither Dan nor Lana replied, Lucas looked up at the general. "Please! I don't want to die! Don't kill me! I was good! I did everything you wanted! Don't kill me, please!"

A sobbing, slobbering mess. Killing him might have been an act of kindness.

The general yanked back on the slide and engaged a round. "Anyone?" he asked Dan and Lana.

"Please, please, please," dribbled from Lucas's lips like his urine from his tattered pants.

"No one?" the general said.

Dan had plenty he wanted to say but stayed shut. Lana offered only more anger, if weaker this time. "He's a fucking kid, you sad bastard."

Bang!

Before anyone had time to see it coming, the general swung the gun down and shot Lucas in his shoulder—grazing him but getting the intended response.

Young Lucas screamed and cried and rolled on the floor in pain, perhaps more imagined than real.

Begged for mercy.

The general handed the gun back to his man, telling Lana and Dan, "How many can he take?"

Dan said, "You didn't have to do that."

"In fact, I did," their tormentor said. "And I will keep doing it. Once a day, at this precise hour, until either one shot is lethal — or I hear what I need to hear."

Dan exploded, showing more fortitude than he should or would have liked. "What the fuck is it that you think we know! What have you dreamed up that we're a part of? We're not goddamned spies!"

The general remained unfettered in his calm. "Yes, you are, and you know precisely what I want to hear."

"No, I do not. I have no fucking clue. We're not fucking spies, you fucking piece'a SHIT!"

The guards stepped closer, hands on their weapons.

Dan backed off.

The general said, "All you have to do is tell me the truth, and Lucas lives."

Lucas shouted, "Jesus, Dan! Tell them! Tell them so they'll let us go!"

Lana said softly, "They're never going to let us go, Lucas."

"What?!" Young, simple Lucas could not wrap his head around that concept. "But you said…. Just TELL them so we can go HOME!"

"We're not going home, Lucas," Lana said. "We're going to die here. I'm sorry."

"No!" he yelled — likely because he knew it was true.

"Lucas," Dan said. Lucas looked over. "Do you know why we're going to die here?" Lucas shook his head no. "Because no matter what we say, they will not believe us. Because what they want to hear, we don't know. Because we're like you, innocent Americans caught up in this…whatever it is, this…war or whatever. And the general here is taking out his frustrations on us because he can. Because he has nothing else. We're going to die because he will never hear what he wants to hear.

"Isn't that right, general?"

A dangerous pall hung in the room—Lucas swinging his head back and forth between Dan and the general. Finally, Lucas said, "See? He doesn't know anything. Nobody does. So you can let us go, right?"

The general had never taken his eyes off, Dan. Finally, he said, "This has gone on long enough."

"You're telling me," Dan said.

"How long do you estimate?" the general said. "Fifteen months? Sixteen?"

Dan hesitated, then said, "Something like that."

The general exploded. "YOU LIE!" He paced a tight circle. "It has been twenty-seven months, and you know it!"

He grabbed the gun again.

"The lying will stop!" he shouted, racking the slide and shooting into the ceiling.

Lucas shuddering and wailing.

The general shouting, "You will tell me why the CIA was operating in my country, what they sought to discover, what they planned to do with that information, and the names of every other agent you worked with here!"

Lana said, "Or what?"

"Or I will kill both your friends slowly in front of you, in the worst possible way you could ever imagine. And it will be *your* fault. Your god will judge you for your inexcusable, pathetic abandonment of your friends. You will burn in hell!"

Lana said, flippantly, "At this point in my life, I think that's already a given."

The general seethed. "Do not mock or test me."

He walked back to Lucas. Grabbed him by the hair and

said to Lana, "One shot at a time. One slice at a time. One body part at a time. Whatever it takes. First, this disgusting excuse for a man — this *boy* — then your lover."

He looked at Dan.

Lucas looked at Dan. "You're *fucking* her? What the fuck, man? We're gonna die in here!"

Dan said only, "Lucas, be quiet. You don't understand this situation."

"I don't have to! That's fucked up! You're sick, you —"

The general pistol-whipped him.

Lucas fell to the floor, whimpering, dazed, apparently having forgotten about the flesh wound to his shoulder.

The general said to Lana, "Your choice. Save them or suffer the guilt."

"I'll die first," she said.

The general laughed. "No," he said. "I will strap you in a cage on an I.V. You will live, and you will watch, and their suffering will be yours."

He fired three shots into the ceiling, causing Lucas to scream with each shot — and his own guards to wince and worry about ricochets — then he said, "Your last warning."

He strode out with the gun.

His men followed their usual routine, backing out, keeping their eyes on the prisoners, then locking the cage door and walking away.

Before their footsteps had faded, the kliegs and horrible metal noise had returned.

Lucas whimpered and wept. It would take hours to get him calmed down this time before Lana would finally doze off. Dan would not sleep.

Something had definitely changed.

30

Things happened quickly from that point on.

In Bethesda, Marion colored her hair—blue. It felt right. She hired an interior decorator and changed the house around, adding curved arches and chair rails, art nouveau ceiling fans and a hot tub. She repainted inside and out and replaced all the appliances and fixtures—again—until she was living in what was essentially a new house.

One without memories.

She did this because she knew she wanted to. She could and, well, why not. Every month, a $15,000 check hit her account. Though the account still had Dan's name on it, no one expected him to make any withdrawals from Beyond.

A ring at the door every few days brought some new accoutrement or gizmo. This day, the Lowes truck pulled up with, "Washer and dryer for a Mrs. Cooper?"

"Ms.," Marion finally felt comfortable saying.

She wore a lower cut top and pondered flirting. Too bad these guys were no more than twenty-three or twenty-four and had so many tattoos they looked like circus performers.

"This way," Marion said, and led them to the freshly-painted laundry room with the new shelves and sink—storage and a built-in ironing board!

"Nice place," the younger one said.

"Thank you," Marion said. "I've been experimenting."

"Everything looks nice and new," the other said. "These units will fit right in. You bought the best we have, that's for sure."

"I hope so," was all Marion felt like adding to the conversation.

The young kid had one more thought. "Must be nice having the cheese to do all this."

Marion did not question the word but did the underlying commentary, "My husband was killed abroad and left me a generous life insurance policy."

The older one said, "Lucky you."

"Yeah," Marion said, suddenly feeling morbidly defeated. "Lucky us."

———————

Deep in the jungle of the North, the general had been keeping his promise.

Each night, in the middle of the night, precisely at three a.m., he interrupted the blaring metal rock and klieg show to shoot Lucas somewhere nonlethal—or have his men kick and beat him—leaving Lucas wailing and begging that they finish the job.

The general would say, "Be careful what you wish for, Lucas. It may be less than you imagine. Or more, depending on your point of view."

And he would leave—until the next night.

He also cut back on their food rations, though none of the

three were likely to refer to the sickening, buggy sludge as food. Sustenance was all it had become, and barely that.

Dan made sure that everyone ate all that was provided, but Lana had taken to vomiting it up at each "meal." Ten days of dysentery — or whatever it was — had left her depleted and wan.

Dan knew he was losing her.

"You have to eat, hon'," he said over every bowl.

"I can't," she would say. Then he would force as many fingerfuls into her mouth as he could before she threw up.

Lucas would groan and turn away. Bitter. "Why do you make me watch that?" he said to Dan. "It's making *me* sick."

"Turn away or go over there," Dan would tell him across the room.

"They shot me like ten times, dude."

"I know," Dan said. "You're doing great. Hang in there."

"Why?"

"Just do it. Eat. Don't look. Pray. Do whatever you have to do, but don't give up."

"*She's* giving up," Lucas said with disgust.

"She can't help it," Dan said.

"Why not? Why can I and she can't?"

"It's just the way it is."

Day after day. If something did not change, some ray of hope, Lana would wither away, and Lucas would either bleed to death from a less-carefully administered "warning shot," as their captor called them, or infection would overtake a wound or several, and Lucas would be gone before Lana.

To keep Lucas going, Dan surrendered the mattress, shifting into the far corner and sleeping on the hard floor with a shivering Lana by the latrine can.

Lucas never thanked Dan or acted thankful, but at least he

slept.

Until the kliegs went off at three a.m., and the general took his ounce of flesh while Lana stared, unable to speak or intervene.

Unable to stop it.

Dan knew that alone might kill her. So, he talked to her, whispering in her ear whenever the music blared loud enough to cover their private conversations — because had the general heard, had he known of the pact being made, he would have killed them all on the spot.

———————

Marion's new Android beeped twice to alert her about an incoming text message from Carlie. The texts had become less frequent, only once a month or so, but Marion's reply remained the same, "I'm fine. Stop texting."

After three glasses of a superb red Sauvignon one afternoon, well before suppertime, Marion took a stroll around her "new and improved home place," as she had taken to calling it in her own mind.

She cocked her head to assess the Calder-like design of the new lighting fixture hanging over the new ten-place Danish Modern dining room set and side table. Everything in the room went with everything else.

What she had always thought she wanted. Now, she had it all.

The Italian red leather sofa and off-white matching chairs in the living room set off the redone fireplace beautifully. The new wall color, divine.

Even the den, a room she had always avoided as it was Dan's workspace, had been reworked to perfection. She got rid of his desk, his computer, and his damned multi-lined phones that rang at all hours of the day and night with instructions to implement this or restructure that some godforsaken place on the far side of the globe.

All gone.

The enormous, curved-screen theatre-style television set would have inspired any visitor — if Marion had any. As it was, she watched old black and white movies in the 4:3 format because it felt old and familiar. Comfortable.

Like sitting in her parents' den in Milwaukee at eight years old.

Other than a major redo on the *en suite* bath, the master bedroom remained mostly as it had always been. Her favorite room before, for its clean simplicity and comfy corner chaise, the low light and quiet middle-back location, Marion changed only the paint — and then only because it needed freshening. The new soft lavender shade proved to be both calming and inspiring — in a non-spiritual way.

Marion's religiosity had long since died a quiet death, and now, so went her spirit.

When she went into her sparkling new kitchen for her fourth wine of the day, something came over Ms. Marion Cooper, and before she knew it, she was pulling her new dishes from the open-style cabinets and hurling them at the stainless appliances and walls.

Next, she threw chairs, tipped over the glass china hutch, and tore down the Calder-inspired floating light fixture until sparks rained down on her and scared her half to death.

After a startled scream and a jump back, as the breaker threw and the late afternoon-set lights went dark, Marion stared at what she had done, disbelieving.

And laughed.

31

Little had been reported in America during the first year of the war so far away. Some news of continuing temblors filtered in for a while — then silence, as if that part of the world had ceased to exist, despite the ongoing conflict. No reports of refugees fleeing, no victim counts, no claims of victories or loss. Nothing.

Then, one day nearly thirty months later, everything changed.

"Breaking News" broke across the full cable spectrum, the internet, and even print. Reports of fighting and casualties in the tens of thousands on both sides arrived in a torrent — without photographic documentation.

Then came news that the president of the South had been shot in the head while sleeping next to his wife. She had been poisoned. No clues were offered as to how anyone could have entered the royal bedroom in the middle of the night, murdered the president and his wife, and escaped unnoticed.

Rumors of executions followed.

The government installed a new president the next day with cautious pomp and ceremony — out of public view. He preferred not to get bombed his first hour on the job. A new cabinet was formed.

New faces.

Immediately, videos of large military deployments flooded newsrooms, followed by allegations of group hangings and long-line firing squads, death trenches and bulldozers — both sides sounding alarms of war crimes and human rights abuses.

The North accused the South of using chemical weapons and requested "United Nations interference," while the South called for "international intervention" to rid the world of the North's weapons of mass destruction — the origins of which were still uncertain.

Within days, global news outlets received a taped message from the new president of the South, a striking man in a fine suit — a young sixty with a younger wife — who did not mince words, demonstrating that he was both articulate and combative.

"The sadistic rebels in the North continue to rain death upon our people with their devious galactic weapon. This is clearly a violation of international protocols and long-standing agreements that has resulted in the deaths of some 200,000 of our people."

He strolled while talking as if making a wine commercial more than calling out an enemy for violating war conventions.

He said, "I implore the global community to end their ignorance of our deep problems and intervene with callous impunity to remove these most dangerous weapons before the barbarians expand their evil across the region and the world."

Shephard Smith came back on to add, "The new president was asked about his side's purported use of chemical weapons but refused to answer, saying only that, and this is a quote, 'We all do what must be done when it must be done. And so the international community must now do what it needs to do.'"

After showing his muted surprise and concern, Shep added, "We are waiting for a joint response from the State Department and the White House."

When that announcement came, it carried the sternest of warnings — the President herself offering the ultimatum to both sides,

"America will not wait for the unnecessary approval from dissenting parties. The civilians in both halves of this war-torn paradise have asked for assistance to end their struggles and stop the killing, and we are going to help."

She turned to a different camera as if the show was *premeditated*.

"At this moment," she said, "a broad international coalition is gathering to provide specific *non*-humanitarian relief."

POTUS Iluwan was flanked by scowling generals — no diplomats.

Within hours, bombs fell. Targets had apparently already been assessed as high-value and were decimated by spent-nuclear-tipped missiles from low-altitude fighter bombers.

Though pilots around the world had for decades reported seeing unidentified aerial phenomena, no UFOs were seen by any pilot in the skies over Phnongtuk; no ground fire was received or detected; no Russian, American, British, or Chinese jets were taken out. The "Joint Attack Program" — with its awful acronym, given the location — was a rousing success.

On television.

On the ground, circumstances proved less clear. For though few lives were reported lost — despite endless barrages of questions from heated-up journalists — the death toll was exceedingly low for such an all-out attack.

The reason was simple, though unreported.

The targets—the Laser beam/UFO hangar in the North and the chemical storage warehouses in the South—were unguarded by soldiers but far from vacant of human life.

Both sides had rounded up the last of their political prisoners, dissenters, and troublemakers, huddled them together in several large groups—thousands on each side—and locked them in the cavernous buildings. Then the JAP force took over.

No one survived.

The world cheered at the pinpoint efficacy of the *warranted* attacks, being told that the dreaded Laser beam machine and internationally decried chemical weapons had been vaporized. (Because the attacks were so complete and overpowering, all-consuming multi-thousand-degree after-fires evaporated any trace of the buildings or purported illegal weapons of mass destruction—much less the actual human contents.)

No reports mentioned alien remains.

With but a few viciously effective air strikes, the weapons, the opposition from both sides and the *history* all ceased to exist in little more than an hour. All that remained were reconciliation talks.

The war was over.

That night in the jungle, when the kliegs went off, and the awful music was muted, the personalized atrocities continued, if later than usual.

The sun was almost up.

This worried Dan more than not knowing what to expect. For if nothing else, the general had stuck to his torture schedule like a diabetic to insulin.

The masked maniac made his entrance just after six a.m.,

waving his own gun around this time, armed guards close and jumpy — their usual dulled attention perked. They shifted their feet and their eyes, nervously trying to assess their cohorts' take on the new situation as the general shouted directions to bring Lucas to him.

Everyone sensed the end of something.

"Tonight, your friend dies," the general said to Dan and Lana. "This is your final opportunity to save his worthless life."

Surprisingly, given the routineness of Lucas's torture patterns, he too seemed aware that this night was different — that his life was truly in danger this time.

"No! Goddammit, NO! Don't kill me. Dan! Lana! Do something! HELP ME!"

With no hesitation, the general racked his weapon, held it close to Lucas's head and fired, taking off part of Lucas's left ear.

Dan yelled, "Hey! That's enough! He doesn't know anything."

"But you do," the general said — and shot off a smaller piece of Lucas's right ear.

While Lucas screamed and thrashed — the guards moving back to allow him room to writhe and bleed — the general said, "Tonight, I am your benevolent executioner."

Lucas wept. Called for Alanda.

His mother.

Lana, who had been quiet — apparently due to her imminent demise — stepped forward unsteadily. "Okay," she said in a weak voice.

Dan said, "No."

Lana said to the general, "You're right. I'm an agent. I'm CIA."

The general smiled. "Of course you are. Continue," he

said.

Lana said, "I'm an operative. ARC was my cover." She took a difficult breath—difficult because her lungs had filled with choking mucus from whatever she had contracted in this hellhole. "But I don't know anything," she said.

The general turned red and fired close to Lucas's head again, eliciting a scream but no blood.

Lana insisted—as much as she was able, "Because I didn't *learn* anything."

"Do you expect me to believe that?" the general said. "You have been lying all along, and you don't lie *now*? You admit you were a CIA operative in my country, but you know nothing?"

This time he shot at Dan! Almost got him!

"Jesus!" Dan shouted as he fell backwards onto the floor, scrambling.

Lucas yelled, "Yeah! Shoot him! Not me!"

The general yelled at Lana, "I will shoot them both if you do not start telling me the truth of all you know!"

"I don't know anything, I swear," Lana said, sagging. "I asked around. I tried to find local sources, but no one would talk to me. I couldn't get anyone to…talk…to me."

She seemed to be fading, perhaps about to collapse.

The general paced, firing off his interrogatories. "What was your assignment? What was your purpose? What was it that you were supposed to be learning that you failed to learn!"

He put the gun to the back of Lucas's head—Lucas shouting, "Tell them! For god's sake! He's going to kill me this time! Tell him!"

"My assignment," Lana said in her weakening voice, "was to gather intelligence on the possible use and development of new weapons in the South that might be used against you in the

North."

The general stopped pacing. "On *us*?" he said—then laughed. "That's ridiculous! Still. You lie!"

He pistol-whipped at Lucas. Fortunately, having been through this so much, Lucas dodged, the muzzle catching only his scruffy blond hair.

"It's the truth," Lana said wearily. "We had intel that the South was developing some new kind of super-powered weapons that could annihilate entire cities if deployed and that your capital was at the top of the list."

The general was flummoxed to the point of stuttering. "But...th...that's absurd. It's *backwards!*"

Dan said, "That's because it is," as he lifted himself to his feet.

The general had no response other than to stare, so Dan gave the answer. "She's not CIA."

Now the general had a response. "And how would you know that?"

"Because she's not your spy. I am."

Lana said, "Dan, no," A soft plea.

"You're lying!" the general hollered. "She is CIA!"

"Nope," Dan said casually. "I am, or was, a CIA operative assigned to gather human-sourced intel on the state of war in your countries—specifically the South. My code name is Diehard, and my 'employment number' is 63454. Right outa Langley—where I used to live while I was training, by the way. Kasner International is a complete front. I'm an agent."

"Bullshit," the general said, violating his own country's language laws.

If he was not convinced, Lucas was livid. He vented at Dan. "You lying sonofabitch. You knew all along, but you didn't say anything? You let them rape me and shoot me? You fucking ASSHOLE!"

Before anyone could stop him, Lucas was up and lunging at Dan—who cast Lucas aside so easily as to make the attack seem laughable, like a four-year-old going after a ten-foot tiger.

As Lucas shook the stars out of his head, Dan said to the general, "Learned skills," and shrugged. To make his point clear, "Would I have been able to do that if I wasn't highly trained?"

The general gave that some consideration, then asked the obvious, "Then why did you not fight before?"

Dan replied like a Valley Girl on Instagram, "Guns much?" He nodded around at the many weapons in the room. "I'm not a fucking idiot," he said. "That's part of the training, too, yeah?"

When he saw Lana wobble, then let go a tiny sigh and slump. Dan took a quick step and caught her—the guards raising their guns at him.

"Don't shoot!" he said. "She's dying. She's not gonna make it."

Lana hung limp, barely breathing, her eyes glazing over.

All the bad signs.

But she had not lost all her defiant spunk. She pulled herself up—still allowing Dan to support her—and said with great effort, "He's lying,"—her eyes partially raised at the general. "He's not fucking CIA. That's a joke."

She scoffed back at Dan behind her. As she did, she lost her footing, Dan catching her as they both fell forward a short step.

She said to the general, "I'm your agent, like I said. Just... take me away. Put me wherever. I'll tell you everything I know. Just...promise you will let these two innocent men go."

The general shook his head. "You have already said you

don't know anything."

"I lied," she said. "And yes, *again*. It's what we're trained to do, yeah?"

"Good try," Dan said from behind her.

"Fuck you," she said. "Fucking liar. You're not CIA material." From somewhere deep inside, she summoned a nasty laugh—which caused her to droop again, her weight pulling them forward as Dan struggled to hold her up. She spat blood.

Dan said, "She's just putting on. Saying that to save my life."

"Fuck. You," Lana said it again and jerked, falling forward again—again, Dan barely catching her as her diminished weight pulled him off-balance another step.

Dan said, smiling, "See? She loves me. She's trying to save me. But the thing is, I love her, too." He looked at Lana briefly with a loving smile, then turned to the general. "You made that happen. And so...you created a problem for yourself."

"What problem?" the general said, snorting contempt. He did not *make* mistakes.

"We will both defend the other to the death and not tell you a damn thing," Dan said.

The general did not hesitate. "Then I will kill your friend Lucas—in front of you both." He aimed at Lucas. "Surely, you would not allow me to kill a truly innocent young man with his entire life ahead of him."

Dan snorted a laugh to match the general's. "What kind of life would he have here?"

The general replied, "Maybe I would let him go. Send him back to America. He is of no use to me. He is not the spy. What do I care what happens to him?"

"Well," Dan said. "To tell you the truth, neither do I."

Lucas perked up. "What?"

Dan spoke only to the general. "Kill him, don't kill him. I don't care." He wrestled Lana's slack body to keep them both standing.

Lucas forced himself to his feet.

Guards stepped closer, raising their weapons as he swore at Dan. "You fucking bastard! I didn't tell them anything about you!"

Dan said, "You didn't *know* anything."

Lucas said, "I could've made shit up! They wanted to kill you! I begged them not to!"

"And thanks for that," Dan said, dryly. Then he turned to the general. "Do whatever you want with him."

"YOU FUCKING BASTARD!"

Lucas lunged again, but the guards caught him. Held him back while he continued to shout invectives—and cry.

"As usual," Dan said coldly.

Then he turned to the general. "Look, here's the deal. You don't need to kill him. He's nobody. You know that. I'm the guy who knows all about the seismic activity sensors, the computer banks, the fake UFOs."

He waited for the general's brow to furrow, then he added, "The whole thing was staged. You had state-of-the-art seismic predictors and had your plan in place for years, just waiting for the first warning of a good-size earthquake, which you then exploited—claiming aliens and superweapons. It was all bullshit to scare the Southies."

Lana said, "Goddammit," and slumped again, looking like she was finally giving up completely—Dan stumbling, barely catching her as she fell forward again. She said, "*I* told you all that! You liar."

She looked at the general. "But I didn't tell him everything." She found a dark smile.

Dan said, "Don't listen to her. I told *her* everything. I'm your man."

Lana's smile evaporated.

The general scoffed. "You are nobody's 'man,'" he said. "Did you think we would not check your history? That we don't have Ask-dot-com? Google? Ya-HOO?" He laughed. "You were never in the military, never in the CIA. You went straight from college to work for Zion Copper, then on to this Krasner corporation. A front for the IMF is what they are, meddling in third world problems. But no connection to the CIA. It's all in the public record."

Dan said, "Of course it is."

His meaning was not lost on the general, whose eyes narrowed. Was his prisoner suddenly being truthful or merely clever?

He decided, "No matter. No one would believe such a story."

"Exactly!" Dan said with surprising enthusiasm. "So you can let us go."

The general threw a snarling laugh.

Dan said, "I have a deal to offer."

"I don't make deals," the general said.

"I think you'll like this one," Dan said. "You'll be surprised."

The general looked unimpressed but said, "Okay. Surprise me, Daniel."

Struggling to keep Lana upright, Dan told him, "Get her to a doctor, and I will tell you anything you want to know. Just...." He choked up. "Just let her live. Get her some help. Medical help.

Help her live."

"No," Lana said weakly.

Dan's eyes seemed redder as he reached around and put his fingers under Lana's chin. "My love. It's the least I can do for you."

He told the general, "Once I know she's safe, that you have saved her life and will set her free, then and only then, I will tell you everything I learned about your program—and theirs. I can help you win your war. But you have to agree to my deal for me to help you."

The general appeared to be thinking through the offer and then said, curtly, "No."

"No?" Dan said.

"She was correct," the general said. "She is going to die. You are going to die. Lucas is going to die. Everyone dies. No one leaves here alive. And do you know why?"

Dan went dark. "No. Why?"

"The war is over."

Lucas said, "What?" and stood up. "It's over? Then why are you keeping us here? How long has it been over? You sick fucking bastard!"

"Mere days," the general said.

Dan said, "So you're just toying with us now."

"Fucking with you, to use your parlance," the general said, gloating. "Yes."

He raised his gun, its muzzle just inches from Lana's nose. A single shot would likely go through her head and into Dan's, killing them both with one shot.

Dan shook his head and chuckled darkly, cynically, knowingly. "Wow," he said. "And you didn't even ask how I was going to surprise you."

"No," the general said. "Although I must admit, I am curious."

"Ah," Dan said—the darkest of smiles coming over his face.

He brought his hands up to gently rub Lana's shoulders, tickling his way up her neck to caress her left temple, to play with a curl of her matted hair.

She giggled softly.

Then he said to her, to Lacey Fremont—as that was her real name—as if cooing to his favorite Valentine, "Shall I, my love?"

"Yes," Lana said, her body relaxing as a genuine smile covered her ashen face. "Do." She held the contentment and looked at the general. The next second….

Dan snapped her neck and let her drop to the floor—dead.

Before the general could process what he had just seen, Dan had his gun and had shot all four guards.

He now ordered Lucas to, "Get their guns."

Stunned stiff, Lucas said, "What? What the fuck did you just DO?"

"Kept a promise. Get their guns. Give me that and that." He pointed with his free hand while keeping the general's gun aimed at the stunned man's face.

The general said nothing, moved not an inch—but his eyes narrowed.

In that moment, something awakened deep inside Lucas's survival-self, and he gathered the guns swiftly.

The general said with surprising calm, "My guards will be in here in seconds—"

Dan ignored him—asked Lucas, "Do you know how to use those things?"

"Sure," Lucas said. Ironically, "They taught me how up at

the Little House."

Good," Dan said. "Shoot anything that comes through that door."

And Lucas did.

The two he missed, Dan took out.

The general stood agape. "What do you think you're doing?"

"Walking out of here, behind you."

As the general began to realize his predicament, he said, "You won't get—"

Bang! Dan shot a piece of the general's ear off—the general wailing in pain.

"Doesn't feel so great when the shoe's on the other foot, does it? To borrow a cliché."

"What?" the general said—unable to hear in that bloody ear.

32

As they stepped out of the cage that had been home for almost two-and-a-half years, Dan immediately felt relief. Though he knew they had a long, dangerous road ahead of them, just getting out of that damned cell, felt liberating.

Before they were out the door, Lucas said, "What was that all about? Why did you...."

"Kill her?" Dan finished for him. "She was dying and knew it. And she knew that if she did tell this fascist fuckbug any of the human intel they learned about him through his defectors in the south—"

"I had no defectors," the general protested. "My men were all—"

"Shut up," Dan told him—and whacked him upside his head with his own pistol. "When I want you to say something, I'll tell you.'

The general huffed. "Talk about clichés."

Dan found it in him to chuckle. "Okay, I'll let that one go, but nothing else."

And thumped him again.

Two guards raced around the corner ahead. Dan had them in his sights and dead before they realized who they were seeing.

"How many more of these loyal yoyos you got?" Dan asked the general—who said nothing. But he did smirk, so Dan thumped him again, warning, "Better be careful. One of those might knock you out, and we'd have to leave you for whoever it is you treated badly."

"They wouldn't dare."

Dan raised the gun. "Wanna give it a shot? So to speak."

The general did not speak.

As they cautiously wended their way through the jungle prison complex, which was much larger and maze-like than Dan had imagined, Lucas asked, "So, everything you said was true about the machines and stuff? It was all *fake*? All they told me?"

"Tell him, general," Dan said. Then to Lucas, "And take that stupid Harley bandana off his face."

Lucas obliged—and recognized him immediately. "You're the guy in the videos—with the beam and...Sur Nam and all that."

Lucas slapped the snot out of the general! Three times! "You lying fuck."

The general sneered but could do nothing more.

Lucas shook his head. "I don't get any of this."

Dan explained quickly as he checked around a corner, saw no soldiers, and shoved the general ahead. "ARC is a front for the Agency, the CIA. They brought agents like Lana in as sales reps or lobbyists to meet businesspeople and politicians to gather information about this asshole and his southern equals."

The general scoffed. "I have no equals in the South."

"Ah, but you do. This whole phony war thing was just an excuse by the North and South to eliminate all your political enemies on both sides, clean up the country and go full-on capitalism. At the end of the day, there will be no more socialists, jihadists, pawns, or meddlers of any sort. And you, my cruel tormenter, will be as dead as they are—all according to plan. Just not yours."

The general bit his tongue.

Lucas said, "So, I still don't, um.... What does this all mean?"

Dan said, "It means, Our country agreed to stay out of this country because people like the general let America know what they were doing and that we, America, would, *will*, profit the most on the aftermath—oil, natural gas, zinc, precious stones. Our corporate thieves and their Euro counterparts will create the illusion of having allowed, or even helped, to create a free country through a fierce war. 'Freedom has won, again!'" Dan mocked.

He poked the general. "Yeah?"

"Close enough," the general said begrudgingly. Then he added, "And those close secret alliances will protect me—and not you."

"We'll see," Dan said, having reached the front gate of the prison, which lay wide open. No need for security out here.

While he considered their next move, Dan finished his summary assessment. "This whole elaborate prisoner of war thing was about keeping Lana quiet until the fake war was over. Then they could kill her or release her. It wouldn't matter. It was all a done deal. In the meantime, she was a chit."

That said, Dan had his plan. "Okay," he told the general. "You first."

With that, he shoved the general out the open door, "Hey! Assholes!" and whistled loudly.

As the general's eyes went wide, thinking he would be

shot by his own men, he dove for the dirt. Dan stuck two full ARs out the wide portico and fired in both directions at once, two long bursts — *then* he looked.

Dead guards at each end.

Now, he and Lucas stepped outside. Dan told Lucas, "Get him up."

Lucas did, roughly, and the general finally began to tone down his defiance. "Perhaps, we can negotiate. I can help you remove yourself from this…sticky situation."

"Out of the kindness of your heart," Dan said, recalling every battery blast to his balls, every sexual assault on his fellow agent he was forced to witness, every brutalization of poor Lucas that he had imagined then heard after the fact — then witnessed.

He turned to the general. "Twenty-nine months, sixteen days, nine hours and sixteen minutes." Just to make it clear as to who knew what.

Then he shot the general through his face and out the back of his head — with his own gun.

Lucas looked down at the mess — and spat.

Dan said, "Where's the Little House? Do you remember?"

"Sure," Lucas said. "How could I forget?" He led the way.

Ten minutes of trekking through the dense sound-muffling jungle later, the Little House came into view — an actual small house in the middle of nowhere.

"Who do you figure is in there?" Dan said, as they peered from behind a thick stand of wild banana trees.

"A few cooks, a maid, some hookers."

"Mostly women?"

"All women."

"Okay," Dan said. "Where are the soldiers?"

"Around the other side," Lucas said. "In their barracks."

"Road out?"

"By the barracks."

"Vehicles?"

"Trucks, usually. Two or three. Maybe a Jeep. Bulldozer."
Dan thought quickly.

The house was small, and the jungle close. He pointed. "You go around that way. Make sure they don't hear you coming. Then get their attention. I'll be on the other side, behind them."

He pointed, Lucas nodded, and they went their separate ways.

Half-a-minute later, Lucas bravely stepped out into the small clearing between the Little House and the barracks, where four soldiers were talking, laughing, and smoking by the bulldozer, a five-ton truck, and a military jeep with a .50 cal in the back.

"Bum a smoke?" Lucas said as if walking up to them by a San Diego beach lifeguard stand on a warm July day.

The guards turned towards him, unsure of what was happening—what to do. He had been a prisoner, if a well-treated one, but had been relegated to the torture chamber with the others weeks ago and—

Dan opened fire from the other side, killing them all in under four seconds—one apiece. "Keys," he said to Lucas.

"In the ignitions," he said, remembering, "They leave them in."

As Lucas climbed into the jeep next to Dan, he asked, "Where are we going?"

"Away from here," Dan said. Then he had another thought. "I'm sorry about what happened in there with Lana. It wasn't easy. But it was what she wanted."

"I understand," Lucas said. Then he opted for honesty.

"Well, not really, but…she's in a better place than that shithole."

Dan shoved the little Jeep in gear, and they were off — to where he was not sure.

33

When Marion Cooper got wind through the Mayers that something was happening again "over there," she turned on CNN to catch Wolf Blitzer in mid-report.

"A coalition of international inspectors pored over the scenes of two recent coalition strikes."

The screen cut to a scene of blackened rubble — total annihilation — as hazmat-suited inspectors pored over the flattened remains of what might have been an industrial complex.

Wolf said, "In the South, inspectors found traces of Sarin, the principle ingredient used in chemical weapons. And in the North...."

The image cut to a similarly minimized pile of black nothingness where a similar group of protection-suited inspectors ran radiation detectors and other strange equipment over the remains of what was apparently the northern hangar from before. Some of the scientists delicately removed tiny samples, securing them in airtight, heavy-duty glass containers with lead shielding.

"...inspectors say they have discovered metallic elements known previously to exist only on *space material* collected from *meteor particles.* Currently, there is no explanation as to how the space material got to Earth."

After some other images played out for the umpteenth time, Wolf returned to say, "Damnedest story I've ever reported."

As usual, his face did not reflect his astonishment.

He turned to the four reporters across from him, all of whom seemed equally confounded and bemused and said, "Panel?"

Marion joined them in their confusion, if with less interest, switched off the TV, and headed for the Miracle-Gro — her new geranium was coming along — so she missed the same Congresswoman being cornered on the Capitol steps by reporters.

"Is it true the materials found in the North could have been placed there by the inspectors themselves?" one asked.

Representative Irene Maudler said she had "no knowledge" of that.

"But it is very similar to materials found at a meteor crash site in New Mexico, is it not?" another reporter offered.

Congresswoman Maudler had no information on that notion either or the results of any investigations "other than what has previously been released." She thanked them and scampered back for her office in the Rayburn Building.

They chased her the whole way.

Later, the White House press secretary held a press conference to tell the press that she did not know anything, either, but that she "would refer you to relevant agencies" and left as well.

She appeared to be sweating more than usual.

While Marion Cooper dead-headed Bachelor Buttons, Dan

Cooper was speeding through the jungle in a jeep stolen from the Army of the North, still not certain he believed the dead general about the war being over — or if it was, if the troops knew.

Lucas reflected Dan's concerns. "What if they find us?"

"Let's hope they don't."

"But what if they do?"

"Shoot back while I try another road."

Lucas pointed out a problem with that plan, "I haven't seen any other roads."

Dan said nothing and kept their speed up as best he could.

Lucas asked, "Where are we going?"

"Home," Dan said.

Hoped.

"Are you really CIA?" Lucas asked with surprising calm. Apparently, the fresh air and sunshine had lifted his spirits.

Not being tortured or shot anymore.

"No," Dan said.

Lucas looked over.

"OCS. Black-Ops," Dan said. "About the same, but a little more…covert."

"Have you killed a lot of bad people?"

"Just the one," Dan said, and smiled.

"And his guards," Lucas said. Thinking back, he added, "Some of them weren't bad. Just guys in the army, I guess."

Dan glanced over but had no comment either way. Lucas was a nice kid who had reeked of white privilege. Gated communities. No way could such a sheltered young man have been prepared for any of what had happened to him. Aside from the PTSD, Dan wondered how all of it would impact the rest of Lucas's life.

"I can't wait to see Alanda's face when I walk in," Lucas

said, grinning.

"*If* you walk in," Dan said.

"Yeah," Lucas conceded. "We're not out of the woods, yet. So to speak." And he laughed at his little joke.

Dan said, "That was pretty good," impressed with Lucas's moment of detachment—encouraging.

Wondering if it would last.

"I guess that's kind of awesome," Lucas said. "You being all secret-agenty and stuff." He pondered the work. "Black Ops. I thought that was just a TV thing. I didn't know it was real."

"It's real," Dan said. "Unfortunately."

Lucas nodded as if he understood the depth of that concept, then said, "Where do you think they'll send you next?" Then he thought back a minute. "If we get out of this."

Dan said, "I think this is my last tour."

"It's been pretty rough," Lucas said.

"Yeah."

Lucas thought back. "So, all that stuff Lana said was a lie? Just making stuff up to try and save us?"

"No," Dan said. "She was CIA. ARC was her cover."

"So, you knew she was an agent?"

"Not at first," Dan said. "I wasn't sure what the hell she was." He chuckled.

Lucas thought back. "Yeah. She was pretty hot in that tiny top that day. Then she just came out of nowhere to help us."

"And get us kidnapped," Dan pointed out.

"Yeah," Lucas said, sadly. "Maybe she didn't mean that part."

"She didn't," Dan said. "But she had an idea who I was even if I didn't know who she was. I hadn't been told yet who my contact was going to be. And I have to admit, I did not expect anyone like her."

Lucas wondered, "Was she even dying?"

"Oh yeah," Dan said. "She was sure of it. That's why I agreed—the only reason I agreed."

Lucas remembered, "She had blood coming out of her mouth."

Dan chuckled. "Yeah, that part. She bit her tongue so that she'd have blood in her mouth to spit out." He shook his head with admiration. "Strong lady. Inspiring." Then he choked up a bit. "Too bad she had to go that way—just fade away to nothing."

"Yeah," Lucas said. Then probably to change the subject, he asked, "What was your assignment? I mean, if you can tell me."

Dan smiled, while ducking a slapping low limb. "Yeah, no. But it wasn't who we ended up with, I can tell you that."

"He was a surprise," Lucas said, nodding. "Fucking asshole. Dead asshole. Motherfucker."

Dan regarded Lucas briefly then, seeing a crossroad ahead, checked on the position of the sun, and chose left.

South.

Lucas said, "Did you love her? Lana. I mean, for real?"

Dan's body tensed and then relaxed as he made the turn. "Yeah. I did."

"Did you think you would?"

"No."

"Are you glad you did?"

Dan drove on in silence.

———

After what seemed like a long trek down the dirt road that became increasingly tight—leading Dan to believe he had chosen poorly—a last cluster of overhanging branches that just about took the remaining paint off the jeep gave way to a sudden opening—and active troops in the near distance, traversing an armored vehicle-launched bridge.

Dan reacted quickly, spinning the wheel and plowing into a thatch of tall grass. He turned off the key, leapt up, and told Lucas to, "Stay put."

He disappeared into the grass.

Dropping to his stomach, Dan slithered through the last of the undergrowth to get a better view, but they were too far away to read any markings.

"Need these?"

Lucas's voice came from right behind him, causing Dan to jump—and wonder how Lucas had snuck up on him.

"I followed you," Lucas said. "I wasn't about to sit there alone."

Dan grimaced, but took the binoculars. "Thanks," he said—and peered down at the troops on the river crossing.

Lucas said, worried, "Do you think they saw us? I don't wanna go back to the place, Dan."

"Don't worry," Dan said, putting down the field glasses. "They're ours."

"Ours?" Lucas said. "Americans?"

Dan nodded, and Lucas was on his feet, running for the deep ravine, shouting, "American! USA! USA! AMERICAN!"

Dan grinned and followed.

———————

The Army Lieutenant assigned to debrief Dan and Lucas in Phnongtuk—after their individual interviews—seemed anything but understanding of their tale. "What the fuck were you two doing way up in there to begin with?"

Lucas took strong exception. "We were kidnapped, asshole!"

Being a civilian.

Dan chuckled.

Their debriefer, a humorless young Lieutenant, said, "You were reported missing and dead in the earthquake."

Dan said, calmly but with an edge, "We heard it wasn't an earthquake."

The Lieutenant said without hesitation, "Well, you heard wrong."

He looked at the papers in the file he was given. "Says here your wives witnessed you being swept away by the tsunami."

Lucas said, "We were kidnapped, buttfuck. They shoved us in a truck and drove us away into that fucking hellish shithole in the jungle. We told you that, you fucking pea-brained dickwad!"

Dan busted a laugh.

The Lieutenant glowered. "Kid, you call me that one more time and—"

"And what, Lieutenant?" Dan said. "A civilian prisoner of war headed back to face the cameras all across America? They still have MSNBC, right? He'd be a good get."

"We'll see about that," the young officer said. He shuffled the papers. "Kidnapped and tortured for more than two years," he said, doubtful. "You look fine to me."

Lucas jumped up—Dan barely holding him back. "You think this looks 'fine'?" He pointed to his newly bandaged ears. "You wanna see my raped asshole, you fuckin' shit-for-brains?"

"Easy, Lucas," Dan said. "It'll all work out. Be patient. He's just doing his job."

"Yeah, well, he's shitty at it," Lucas said, and sat back down.

Dan said, "Lieutenant, why don't you try being a bit more...sympathetic. We've been through a lot."

"Yeah," Lucas said. "Over two years of that shit. You try it, 'Lieutenant.'"

"He's got a point," Dan said.

The Lieutenant buried his face in his paperwork—probably mulling over the many things he *wanted* to say.

Dan knew the type, and even the situation. "Look," he told the young man. "Ask us whatever you like. We'll tell you the truth. But think about this, Why would we lie about anything like that?"

The Lieutenant said, "You're 'Special Black Ops,' you tell me." He made it clear that he thought this was ridiculous.

Lucas shook his head, woeful, and said, "You know what's stupid? You."

When the Lieutenant glared at him, Lucas snorted. "He can pop your neck like nothing." He demonstrated. "Without breakin' a sweat. Maybe you should be nicer."

Not one to be intimidated, the Lieutenant said, "Speaking of that, what about this Lana Morrison?"

"That's the name *you* gave her," Dan said." *She* said it was Lana Yarborough. Or Lacey Fremont. But none of those may have been her real name," Dan said. "I'm sure the Agency won't confirm or deny any of them."

The Lieutenant said, "CIA's never heard of her. ARC has never heard of her. No one's ever heard of her."

Dan said, "There's a surprise."

The Lieutenant heaved a sigh. "Look, Dan, or whatever *your* name and...job is, I'm just here to make sure everything's copacetic and get you back to life in the U.S., okay?"

"Then act like it," Dan said.

The Lieutenant dropped his file. "What do you want me to do? Huh? Believe everything you say on the face of it? Sounds pretty wild if you ask me."

Dan said, "Compared to UFOs and aliens?"

The Lieutenant demurred. "I'm saying, none of you—except *him*—seem to exist at all." He made sure to slur Lucas. "And he's nobody."

"Fuck off," Lucas said. "Dan's here, and Lana was there—or whoever she is. Was. Check her DNA or her fucking teeth or something. Fingerprints. Show someone a picture of her dead fucking face."

Somewhere along the line, Lucas had gotten some balls—or lost all patience.

"Yeah," the Lieutenant said. "If we had that, we would."

"What do you mean?" Lucas said. Then turned to Dan. "What does he mean?"

Dan said, "He means she wasn't there when they went to check out our story."

Lucas turned back to the Lieutenant. "What do you mean she wasn't there? Dan broke her neck and left her there. Then he killed the general and, like, a dozen guards and shit."

Dan thought, *Nice, Lucas. Thanks. That should help.*

The Lieutenant did not care. "Yeah, well, she wasn't there. No one was." He glared at Dan—just in case. "'The general'?"

Dan said only, "Marshal stars on his collar."

Lucas said, "He's the one who shot my fucking ears off. Dan popped him in the face and left him there to rot."

"With the dozen soldiers," the Lieutenant said, sounding doubtful with full intention.

"Yeah," Lucas said.

"And the spy lady with the hot body. Broke her neck

because he loved her," the Lieutenant said — staring at Dan while talking to Lucas.

Lucas now heard his own words being said back to him. "Maybe I shouldn't'a said all that, but yeah. That's what happened. So why are you pretending it didn't?"

"Because," the young Lieutenant said, leaning forward. "We *did* go there, and we did check it out. Thoroughly, I can assure you. And it matched what you said, building for building, room for room."

"So? There's your proof," Lucas said, exasperated.

Dan said, understanding, "It was clean."

"Bingo," the Lieutenant. "Not one body, not one drop of blood."

"That's impossible," Lucas said. "It was all over the place."

"Scrubbed," Dan said. And asked, "What about the racks and batteries. Torture devices."

"There weren't even any locks. Just open cells and half-rotten old wooden doors. Place looked like a run-down B&B. Other than that, it was as clean as an expensive whore's pussy at the beginning of the night. You could eat off the floor."

Dan was uncertain about the Lieutenant's mixed metaphor, but Lucas had other issues, "You must've gone to the wrong place. It's out in the middle of nowhere."

The Lieutenant said, "Nope. Dan here gave very precise coordinates, considering, and it matched your descriptions perfectly — except for the rest of your story."

"Well, it all happened," Lucas said, sullenly. "Did you take pictures, at least?"

"Sure did," the Lieutenant said, and retrieved them from his folder. Sure enough, the old prison was spotless and empty.

Dan shook his head — found it in him to chuckle.

The Lieutenant softened. "You see my dilemma?"

"I do," Dan said.

"I don't," Lucas said. "What the hell happened?"

Dan said, "They came in after us and cleaned it up as if we were never there. As if no one was ever there. You ever see *Pulp Fiction*. Mr. Wolfe?"

"Oh yeah," Lucas said. "That was cool." Then he thought about it. "But...so now it's like none of it happened?" Lucas said. "None of what they did to us?"

"Nada," Dan said, speaking Southern Californian to Lucas

"That's fucked up," Lucas said and sat back to be amazed.

"Sorry, fellas," the Lieutenant said, standing and gathering his paperwork.

"What now? Dan asked.

"I want to see my congressman," Lucas said, having no idea who that was.

The Lieutenant said, "That won't be necessary. I'm gonna turn you over to Sgt. Aaronson, who will finish your in-country debriefing. When he's done, you'll be transferred to Diego Garcia to answer a few more questions — after we've had a chance to run down some of this." He held up a tape recorder.

"Then what?" Lucas said belligerently.

"Then you go home," the Lieutenant said. Then he turned to Dan. "Good job, sir."

Tired, Dan said, "We're alive."

The Lieutenant said, "Like I said." He turned to go. "And good luck, gents."

Then he was gone.

"What was that?" Lucas said, stumped.

"He was just testing us," Dan said. "Make sure our stories held up."

"Great," Lucas said. "We have to prove what we went through."

"Welcome back to America," Dan said. "The long way around."

When they looked up, Sgt. Aaronson was approaching them with papers to sign, cold Cokes, Bugles and Doritos, and a big smile.

The good cop.

––––––––

The flight to Diego Garcia was smooth, as was the second round of debriefing. There would be more Stateside, but the worst was over. All Dan and Lucas had left to endure was the twenty-two-hour ride back to Edwards, where they were separated.

"Good luck, kid," Dan said as they headed in opposite directions. And he warned him, "They probably don't want us talking about any of this, so this may be the last time we see each other.

"Okay," Lucas said. Then he came back to hug Dan. Tightly. "Thanks, man. I couldn't've...."

"Yeah," Dan said. "Maybe you could. You did good, Lucas. It was tough. Tougher than anything anyone you have ever known or will ever know will ever have to go through. Be proud. Stay strong."

"Okay," Lucas said, tears welling. "But thanks, anyway."

"Sure, kid," Dan said.

He could already taste that steak at Outback to celebrate his early retirement.

34

Quite the storyteller, Alanda's father closed in on the punchline of one of his many "humorous" memories, his grin already stretching ear to ear. "And then, do you know what that rascal did?"

Alanda's mother said, "Tell us, Father."

"He walks over to old Henry —"

"Tomkins," Alanda's mother filled in for accuracy.

"Yes, yes, Henry Tomkins," Alanda's father said, impatiently — dying to get to the hilarious conclusion to his mini-memoir — but took the time to embellish, as was his wont during story time. "Meanest old goat to ever walk through my front door!"

"At the office," Alanda's mother clarified, nodding.

"Of course, at the office," Alanda's father said hurriedly. Then he looked, grinning, at Ashton Mosely, sitting opposite him at the other end of Alanda's dinner table. "And he says —"

"Ashton," Alanda's mother said.

"Yes, yes, Ashton, here," Alanda's father said.

Under the table, Alanda squeezed Ashton's hand, proud

to hear her father telling a story about him as he only told stories about people he adored or hated. Fortunately, Ashton had moved into the former category.

"He said," her father said, "'Henry' — no, wait. I believe he was properly formal, and he said, 'Mr. Tompkins, *sir*, I beg to differ with your assessment of this situation regarding P&G Radionics.'" Alanda's father howled with jovial memories. "You hear that? 'Your assessment of this situation!'"

"To Henry Tomkins," Alanda's mother marveled. "What an absolute scream!"

Her laughter followed her husband's. Alanda's followed hers.

Ashton blushed. "I was just trying to help that situation, sir," he said.

"You were, you were!" Alanda's father decreed, wiping unbridled tears of joy from under the bottom rim of his glasses. "And you did! P&G signed for another year!"

"My, my," Alanda's mother said. "You must be very proud, dear."

She said this to her daughter.

Rather than fawn, Alanda squeezed Ashton's hand again, then retrieved hers to the top of the table before causing a family hemorrhage and said, "I told you Ashton was smart. That he'd be a good fit at Carrollton."

"Well, let's not go too far," her father bellowed. "You'll have him taking my job before we get to dessert!"

His wife found the notion positively hilarious — almost as comical as her husband.

Ashton continued to blush and said, "I don't have my hopes up for that position, sir. Only you will ever be up to command and control at Carrollton, sir."

"Command and control!" Alanda's father roared. "This boy, this *soldier!*"

Alanda muttered, just loud enough for Ashton to hear, "This suck up."

But she was grinning as wide as her dad.

Just as her mother said, "Speaking of dessert, what are we having tonight, dear?" the doorbell rang. Alanda had chosen what she deemed a happy, electronic series of tones, the lead-line from "Knock, Knock, Knockin' on Heaven's Door" — apparently not considering the irony.

Her father gave his usual, "Are you expecting someone, Alanda?" As if it was indecent that anyone should arrive unannounced *at this hour*.

Six-thirty.

The next moment, Alanda saw the unexpected visitor and dropped her just-filled glass of wine on the new hardwood floors.

Lucas, looking ten years older, weary and confused — bandaged — holding a bottle of champagne and a bouquet of twenty-eight red roses — one for each month away from his wife — said, "What's going on?"

In D.C., the late afternoon light was fading as Marion Cooper stepped out the back door to deposit the kitchen trash bag in the large blue can and roll it out to the curb. When the motion-sensor light came on, she froze.

Dan had been standing in the back yard long enough for it to have gone out.

The moment hung in time, filled with history — then she dropped the bag and ran into his arms, Dan taking fast steps to meet and hold her.

In less than two years' time, tourism flourished in the newly repatriated north and south parts of the newly named Botahnah — international visitors ferried around freely in buses with UFOs and happy alien beings painted on the side under the new slogan, *Botahnah – the perfect "space" for a vacation.*

Over 400,000 citizens of the former North-South enemies had died. Capitalism thrived, and all was forgotten.

By law.

Deep in the jungle, a busload of eco-tourists stepped down into the newly paved courtyard of a squat but solid structure with a rebar atrium in the center, surrounded by "nine luxury suites with indulgently sumptuous *en suite* baths."

No buckets in the corners.

The Little House still carried the name The Little House and offered "deluxe accommodations for the discriminating guest."

The same cooks and maids from before catered to their new guests who marveled at the beauty of this most remote jungle eco-lodge. "Such a lovely, peaceful place."

And the dollars rolled in.

THE END

Glenn A. Bruce wrote the hit movie *Kickboxer* and wrote for *Walker: Texas Ranger*, *Baywatch*, the original *G.L.O.W.* Show, and Cinemax's *Assaulted Nuts*. He holds an MFA from Lindenwood University and was an associate professor at Appalachian State University for over 12 years, where he taught Screenwriting, Acting for the Camera, and Video Production, which resulted in several awards for writing and directing. Glenn has had over 50 short stories, essays, and poems published in the U.S., Britain, Canada, Australia, and India. He currently judges a tri-annual short story contest, writes 1-2 screenplays per year, and recently finished his 28th novel.

www.ingramcontent.com/pod-product-compliance
Lightning Source LLC
Chambersburg PA
CBHW050722180626
46814CB00002B/562